Jenny Appleton

A Summerfield Christmas Wedding

A SUMMERFIELD VILLAGE
SWEET ROMANCE

A Summerfield Christmas Wedding
Copyright © Penny Appleton (2020). All rights reserved.
www.PennyAppleton.com

ISBN: 978-1-913321-51-2

For any inquiries regarding this book,
please contact the rights team at Curl Up Press:
www.curluppress.com/contact

Cover and Interior Design: JD Smith Design

www.CurlUpPress.com

Printed by Amazon KDP Print

For my dearest friend, Arnetta

Chapter 1

Patricia Anderson, the new verger of St. Peter's church, scraped her boots carefully before entering the church that she served. Over the centuries, farming families had walked to Sunday service across the fields and arrived with their boots caked in mud. They had used the ancient iron boot scraper outside on the porch, just as Patricia used it now.

It was only a quick walk from Patricia's cottage, but golden September had turned to stormy October. Huge raindrops had crashed onto her large verger's black umbrella. She had walked with it angled against the wind that swept across the churchyard. St. Peter's church was built in the 14th century by the Duke of that time. He owned most of the land around the village of Summerfield and the peasants labored for him in the fields. The only noble family in the village were the Bartlett-Browns, who also owned land and a Manor House.

The population of England was growing at that time. St. Peter's became a sanctuary in times of war, famine, and plague. When the Duke fell in battle, the Bartlett-Brown family took over the maintenance of the church. But after being open for worship through 600 years, the congregation diminished to nothing, and St. Peter's had closed two years before. Retired from her previous job in Oxford, Patricia loved the old church and was excited to be appointed verger. She saw opportunities to make it live again as the center of the village.

Patricia was in her sixties with short, white hair and sparkling, cornflower-blue eyes. There were crinkly laughter lines around her eyes, which made her look cheerful and approachable. A verger in the Church of England holds the ancient role of administrator for a specific parish church. Vergers are appointed to manage everything for the minister to free them for spiritual work. Patricia stood about 5'5" in the historic attire. A high-necked, full-length, black robe fell to her feet, and around her waist was a wide, leather belt with a big ring of keys. The belt and fobs of the keys were stamped with the crossed keys of St. Peter, the patron saint of vergers.

Rain blew against the tower on St. Peter's, staining one side dark-charcoal grey. It was a square tower rising with delicate stonework to a short spire at the top. Stone posts at each corner of the tower held modern lightning conductors. Their stalks, with triangles on top, reminded Patricia of flags in a medieval jousting tournament. She could hear rain pattering on the long, slanting slate roofs below the tower. It gurgled along modern guttering, held in place by the ancient gargoyles with grimacing, devil faces. A notice on the gate to the porch directed worshippers to the parish church of St. Mary the Virgin in the nearby village of Chipping Hanley. There was a warning flyer from Ecclesiastical Security stating there was no lead on the building and that they protected the church with CCTV.

Selecting a key from the bunch in her hand, Patricia unlocked the gate and stepped into the porch. She closed her umbrella, stood it in a corner, and looked up at the noticeboard hanging on the wall.

Two years ago, it had been alive with information about births, marriages, deaths, choir practice, and bellringing.

Now it held only the business card for the Reverend Tim Fell, Minister for both St. Mary's and St. Peter's, with his smiling photo and phone number on it. Patricia knew he was busy with an active parish in Chipping Hanley, but he had promised to come and see her soon. Every day, she greeted his picture with a cheery *good morning!* to remind herself that she had a partner in this venture at St. Peter's. Another heavy iron key opened the massive wooden door of the church and she lifted the iron latch to enter. Patricia switched on the overhead lights. They had been replaced three years ago when the ancient wiring burned out. But there was no heating in the big stone building.

Patricia had completed her training in Oxford and started work two weeks ago. She had shivered continuously. How did other vergers in years gone by keep warm? Ski shops in Oxford suggested silk thermal underwear and leggings that she now wore beneath the traditional robe. Patricia added a pair of fur-lined hiking boots and was now not elegant, but definitely warm!

She looked around at the damp church, which showed the enormous task ahead. Yesterday, she had spent the entire day cleaning and was too tired to assess her progress. Today was for rest and paperwork, so Patricia had come to see how it all looked.

Inside the door, solid walls of local stone rose to a vaulted, wooden roof above rows of oak pews. Beside the baptismal font, someone had tied the bell ropes to nails, high enough to deter idle hands from pulling them. Patricia shuddered and thought that no one would want to touch the furry handgrips sprouting black mold! The wall behind had green spirals growing upward on the damp plaster. But the arched windows on both sides of the church had magnificent stained glass, and she felt a wave of love for St. Peter's, steeped in generations of sacred music, prayer, and service to God. She was fierce in defense of it and determined to help it live again as the center of the Summerfield community.

Patricia crossed the stone floor and walked down the left aisle to the organ. A thick blue rope cordoned off the organ bench and the tarnished pipes needed expert restoration. Where would she find such a person? How would she raise funds to pay for the work? She needed to ask Tim. More urgently, water was getting in somewhere. Rotting floorboards ran from the organ, under the pews, clear to the storage room at the back. Patricia tested each for soundness, and it would all need to be ripped out.

She looked through the open door of the back room. It was a fair-sized room with windows down one side. In it were only two metal chairs with cracked wooden seats and a pile of mildewed hymnbooks. The back door to the church was bolted, and was next to the unpleasant restrooms, which were added in 1912. In her imagination, Patricia saw a Mother and Toddler Group meeting here, on warm, clean carpet, with a reading area snug with beanbags. It would be a safe place for little ones to play and could be a display area for the Sunday school. She believed that Christian outreach would help St. Peter's live again.

Walking back to the altar, Patricia bent to admire the 14th-century ceramic tiles in black and gold she had cleaned yesterday. They were worth the ache in her back, but as always, she stopped and looked up. The stained-glass window above the altar was an inspired piece of glass work. Whoever made it must have been filled with love to design and complete such a piece of work. A life-size figure of Jesus stood in the glow of a candle and Patricia murmured, "Jesus, the Light of the World. '*Follow me and you will never walk in darkness.*'"

In three corners, the glassmaker had placed angels. The top left corner held Michael, the only named Archangel in the Bible, and leader of all the angels. In the top right corner was Gabriel, and in the bottom left was Raphael. The bottom right corner was empty because an angel had fallen.

Yesterday, Patricia had balanced on the stepladder from her cottage and polished this window till it shone. Then she cleaned the altar below and the area around it.

She went into the robing room behind the organ to fetch the new green-and-gold altar cloth Tim had given her. The robing closet held white candles and an upright cross, carved from light oak. Patricia smoothed the green-and-gold runner on the altar, placing the candles and cross directly at the feet of Jesus. After lighting the candles, she switched off the overhead lights and knelt to pray in the front pew.

Patricia smiled as she bowed her head over interlaced fingers. Old English words fascinated her, and her knees rested on a *hassock*. This meant *a clump of grass* in old English. This one was tatty and faded like all the rest. Might some people enjoy a morning of tapestry, with coffee and prayers? She watched the candle flames flicker in the reds and blues of the stained glass. The next event in the church calendar was the Feast of all Hallows, known more commonly as Halloween. After that came Advent and Christmas. None of them would be celebrated at St. Peter's this year.

Patricia would sing with the choir at St. Mary's. Would this Christmas be as lonely as last year? Patricia closed her eyes.

Dear Lord, please help me to do better. I am so grateful to be fit and well, with enough energy on most days. There are some days when I feel ninety and depressed. But I put myself in this isolated position when I moved to Summerfield.

I miss Paul, Charlotte, and Amber. I tried with Eve for a long time, but she made it clear that Paul is her husband before he is my son. I feel that I have lost him. I have so many blessings, but no family to share them with. Please help me to count my blessings and contribute at St. Peter's.

Patricia thought back five years, to when she nursed her husband, Ron, through the last months of his life. He died of cancer and she had wanted to sell the big house in Oxford as fast as possible. Paul, Eve, and the girls, Charlotte and Amber, lived nearby and Paul did not want her to sell. "Leave it for a while, Mum. Everyone says you should wait a year."

Patricia had loved helping with her granddaughters when they were young. But now they were teenagers and did not need her. Speaking with Paul, she fought off another panic attack. "I feel so desperate in that house. I go around and around on all the memories. I need to get away, live in a smaller place, and do something different."

Patricia found distraction in hard work and before retirement, had many projects. The money came through from the sale of the house and she bought two joined Victorian cottages in Summerfield. They needed renovation, and she had enjoyed living in Number 1 while she worked on Number 2. She had always dreamed of living in the country and having a dog of her own. She had found Sophie at the canine rescue center, volunteered in the office at Summerfield Stables, and made new friends. Over time, the fog of grief had lifted, but family relations remained chilly.

Patricia dropped her hands from her face and gently twisted the wedding band around her finger. Last Christmas showed that she was not needed nor wanted. But it was not time for a pity party. She pushed away the sad thoughts, found a tissue, and wiped her face.

Stop it now. Lots of older folk live away from their families and will be alone over Christmas.

Clair, her friend from the Stables, had called yesterday and invited her for coffee. Patricia had been too busy cleaning, but decided she would go today. She felt lighter as she stood up and whispered, "Thank you. I shall snuff the candles and lock up. I will go get Sophie, change, and walk to Stables Cottage."

Chapter 2

Sophie was waiting for Patricia inside the front door of the cottage, her feathery tail waving like a flag.

Dog lovers say their dogs understand every word they say, and Patricia was certain this was the case with Sophie. She was a four-year-old English setter, with a long, white coat that had big splashes of black in it. She had a sweet face and expressive black eyebrows, but was prone to anxiety. When Sophie ran, she was a picture of beauty and joy. Silky ears flapped wildly, the long coat streamed out behind, and her tongue hung out of the corner of her mouth. Sophie had sympathetic eyes that watched Patricia now. "Hello, Sophie, are you ready for your walk?"

Patricia went upstairs to change, and Sophie followed. They had many conversations in which Patricia spoke human English and Sophie replied with body language. She was Patricia's dearest companion. "I am never lonely with you around. I am so lucky to have you."

Sophie galloped down the stairs and into the kitchen. She sat next to her harness and leash. Patricia smoothed her long fur and fitted her harness.

Patricia now wore a cream shirt and sweater with stone-washed denim slacks. It was still chilly but the rain had stopped and there were flashes of blue sky. Patricia tucked the folding umbrella into her backpack, just in case. She slipped on her green gumboots and a new red quilted coat she had bought in Oxford. She added a white beanie hat with a silky pom-pom, then chuckled as she looked in the hall mirror. Clair would say something about her looking Christmasy already.

It was a twenty-minute walk from Halfmoon Cottages to Summerfield Stables via the back lane. Patricia swung into a rhythmic stride, and Sophie ran out on the extending leash. The highlight last Christmas had been the Nativity pageant. She had worked with Clair, who co-owned the Stables and ran the *Riding with Challenges* program. Patricia recruited Tim Fell to be the Narrator and St. Mary's choir to lead the carols. With Staff, students of every ability, and all the horses and ponies, they had enacted the Christmas story. It was the most moving Nativity Patricia had ever seen.

"We must stay cheerful, Sophie. It is the time of year for bright Christmas lights, comfort food, and lots of sleep. I am feeling unlovable, so must focus on helping others. Sometimes, in unexpected moments, love shines through the darkest places."

The Stables looked lovely in the sunshine. They had been constructed in sand-colored stone on three sides of a square, enclosing a cobbled courtyard. There were stalls for twenty horses and ponies and, in the old Duke's time, a coach and pony cart. The fourth side of the square had an archway with the year, *1743* carved over the top.

In front of this was a wide parking lot with a smooth surface for wheelchairs to travel easily into the stables. The whole facility was wheelchair-friendly with the working part of the Stables around the side and back, where trucks brought loads of hay and took away manure. The farrier worked in the yard there, trimming pony feet and shoeing horses.

Patricia crossed the parking lot and glanced into the yard. She waved to a volunteer who was bringing a white pony to the mounting block. Opening an arched door into the walled yard of Stables Cottage, Patricia slipped through with Sophie.

This cottage was big and rambling, with thick walls, painted a pale pink. Tiny windows peeped from beneath a straw-thatched roof. Stables Cottage had been the home of the Duke's Head Coachman for centuries, the last of whom was Clair's grandfather Ted. The mature garden had an orchard of apple and pear trees. Under them was Ted's pride and joy, a long chicken run with Rhode Island red hens and a rooster.

Clair opened the door at Patricia's knock and gave her a big hug. "Thanks for coming! I was beginning to think I could not seduce you from the charms of the new job. You look jolly in that red coat and green boots, like one of Santa's elves!"

Patricia hugged Clair back. "I don't know whether that is a compliment, but thank you anyway! How do you manage to wear so few clothes and not feel the cold?"

Clair was thirty years younger than Patricia, but the age gap was not a barrier. Friends are the family you choose for yourself. They had shared trials and tribulations over the two years that Patricia ran the Stables Office.

Clair Williams had married David Bartlett-Brown in the summer and now they jointly owned and managed Summerfield Stables. Clair was in her early thirties, tall, and athletic with short, curly hair and golden-brown eyes. She was wearing stylish black riding pants, tall boots, and a short-sleeved shirt with the Summerfield Stables logo on the top pocket. Patricia loved her and wished she had a similar relationship with her daughter-in-law. Sophie pushed her nose into Clair's hand, waving her silky tail.

Clair squatted to stroke the elegant head. "Hello, gorgeous girl." She looked up at Patricia, "I am on a break between teaching classes. Before you take off your coat, would you like to pick up windfall apples with me? We can have coffee after that."

Patricia accepted a wicker basket from a peg by the front door. "I have some blackberries in the freezer; I could make a pie."

Clair shut the cottage door behind them. "David is going to make apple crumble for dessert."

Clair did not enjoy cooking, but David was keen on it.

"Jossie is in with Granddad."

Patricia thought of Ted's Springer spaniel dog, who normally came out to play with Sophie. "What's up that you don't want Ted to overhear?"

Clair stared at her, "I miss you. You pick up vibrations so quickly. It's Granddad I'm worried about."

Patricia was glad of gumboots in the long grass and ducked under branches to avoid drips down her neck. Clair had lived at Stables Cottage with her grandparents since she was thirteen. Her parents and young brother had been killed in a motor accident. Ted and May Williams, her grandparents, had brought her up, but May had died before Patricia joined the Stables.

"What is it that is worrying you?"

Off leash, Sophie puttered around the chicken run, and Clair began to collect apples to fill her basket. "He is getting frailer, and with the Stables, we are struggling. David helps him dress every morning, but he gets breathless and I cannot keep coming back over from the arena to check on him. But he gets mad if I suggest going to the doctor."

Patricia laughed. She understood Ted's determined spirit and wish for independence. She had been away in Oxford on her verger's training course and felt Clair's fear of losing him. "How can I help?"

"His heart tablets seem to be less effective. You are a friend Granddad respects and he might go to the medical center, if you thought he should. Could you pop in and see him?"

Patricia added another rosy apple to her basket. "I cannot stay today but I could come again tomorrow."

"That would be great!"

Patricia picked up a big russet apple and sniffed it. "This has a heavenly scent."

Ted and May had planted an orchard of Oxfordshire heritage fruit trees when they were first married. She was about to take a bite when she spotted the bruised part and a worm. "Ah, this is one for the chicks!"

Patricia threw the apple high into the air, over the mesh fence and in among the poultry. Twelve hens ran clucking for the apple and Patricia turned to Clair, laughing, but her friend seemed pre-occupied. "Is something else bothering you?"

Claire shrugged her shoulders, "It feels disloyal to talk about it, but Audrey is having problems in the office. She is enthusiastic but struggles with the computer."

Patricia chuckled. "*She* struggles? *I* struggled with that old thing! Could your budget stretch to buy a new one now? And some new software? I could come to the office after I see Ted if you like. I updated the processes before I went but I might be able to help Audrey."

Clair looked happier as she picked up her full basket. "That would be wonderful, and I will talk with the team about a new computer. Are you ready for coffee now?"

Patricia's basket was only half full. "I will be in the car tomorrow so I will pick up a few more and take them then. Call me when the coffee is ready."

Clair carried her basket to the back door of the cottage, slipped off her boots, and went in. Sophie came over to sit near Patricia and scarcely a minute later, the arched door to the stable yard slammed back hard against the wall. Startled, they both turned to see a huge black dog, as big as a wolf, bounding down the path toward them. It had white scars on its sides and ragged ears. Patricia dropped the basket and grabbed Sophie. Apples bounced all around them, but the dog flashed past them, its eyes fixed on the hens.

A deep male voice shouted, "Hannibal!"

Patricia's head turned to see the owner of the voice. The dog hit the chicken wire, bounced off, and raced along the side, barking furiously. Hysterical hens raced for the hen house as Rocky the Rooster flew to defend them. The dog stood on its hind legs and pawed the wire mesh as Rocky pecked viciously at him.

Chaos bounced off the walls as a stocky man with grey hair and a white beard hurried down the path. "Hannibal, DOWN!"

The dog dropped to the ground as Clair, minus her boots, came running out of the cottage. Patricia recognized Anthony Bartlett-Brown, David's brother, Clair's brother-in-law. She had met Anthony at the Nativity ride, at the lease auction, and when he was best man at Clair and David's wedding, but she'd never seen the dog. Then she remembered. Hannibal must be the military sniffer dog Anthony had rescued from being put to sleep.

David lost a leg in an Afghanistan explosion, but Hannibal's warning had saved his life. The dog was returned to the UK with the other injured vets, but no one would adopt him because he was big and damaged. Anthony adopted him in the nick of time.

Now, he reached Hannibal and clipped a short leash onto his harness. "I opened his crate in the back of the car and he jumped past me before I could grab him. I am so sorry."

Together, they walked over to examine the chicken wire.

Patricia abandoned her apples and sat down on the bench with Sophie. While she waited for Clair, she observed Anthony. He and David did not look like brothers, having the same father, Sir George Bartlett-Brown, but different mothers. Clair told Patricia that Anthony at sixty, was the son of George's first wife who had died of tuberculosis when Anthony was a young boy. David's mother was Nancy, an American who had married George, found him impossible to live with, but had two children before she divorced him. She went back to America and now lived in California with David's sister.

David stood over six feet tall and was dark, athletic, and a former soldier. Anthony was twenty years older, about 5 feet, 7 inches tall with a more rounded figure. Patricia had first met him while he was still working in the City of London. He had been professionally dressed in an immaculate business suit with white shirt and silk tie.

Today, Anthony was wearing baggy blue jeans, a chunky, brown knit sweater, and sports shoes. His grey hair was receding, but Patricia liked his twinkling brown eyes and beautiful voice. He had given a splendid performance as Santa Claus at the end of Clair's Nativity pageant last Christmas. Patricia had been singing with the choir as he arrived in the pony cart decorated as a sleigh and gave out Christmas candy from his pack. He seemed a nice man and she had been sorry he lived in London because St. Mary's choir could do with that beautifully modulated bass voice! But Clair said Anthony was moving back to live in Summerfield, since adopting Hannibal.

The last time they met was six months before at Clair and David's wedding. Anthony was the best man, and it was Patricia's first event as trainee verger at St. Peter's church. He had complimented her on how well she had organized everything, then disappeared back to London again.

Clair's grandfather, Ted came hobbling from the cottage, leaning on his cane. Patricia was shocked at the change in him. Ted was eighty-something and of small build, but his sheepskin coat hung off him, and he looked unwell.

Anthony pulled at the neck of his sweater like a schoolboy. "I'm sorry about that, Ted. Hannibal has not been trained around chickens."

The black dog lay quiet, and Ted stared at the pile of terrified hens beneath the hen house. "Those were bred from the last of May's hens. They have heart attacks if they are stressed. My dog went berserk inside. If he had been out here there would have been one hell of a dogfight."

Anthony began to apologize again, but Ted raised a hand and started back up the path. He was breathless. "No eggs for a week, that's for sure."

Clair caught up to him and he took her arm. They went back into the cottage. Anthony was left standing awkwardly in the middle of the yard.

Patricia tied Sophie to the bench, in case Hannibal was aggressive, and went over to speak to him. "Hi! Good to see you again."

He held out a hand to shake. "Hello again. Sorry about the drama. I'm moving back to Summerfield today and that was not a good start. I'll put Hannibal back in the car and straighten the chicken wire for Clair. Back in a few minutes."

Hannibal walked obediently to heel out of the gate toward the parking lot, and Clair returned wearing her boots. Patricia had picked up the basket but decided to leave the apples. She told Clair where Anthony went, and Clair bent to untie Sophie's leash.

"Thank goodness none of the hens are dead or we would never hear the last of it from Granddad. I have not even had the chance to ask how are things going at St. Peter's?"

Patricia hesitated, "Tim is busy in Chipping Hanley parish and it's lonely, compared to working here. But we have our first planning meeting next week. I have tons of ideas and it is exciting to have a project of my own. The tenants arrive in the cottage next door on Saturday, and it will be great to get to know some new people."

Anthony came back and indicated that he would check the hen run. He began to stretch Hannibal's shape out of the wire and Clair looked at her watch. "I was going to show Anthony the Stables Loop through Potlatch Wood, but I'm teaching in six minutes. Any chance you could take him?"

Patricia put on her backpack. "Sophie and I walked down the lane to here. We could walk back through Potlatch Wood to show Anthony the route."

Anthony smiled as he joined them and heard what Patricia said. "It was a long drive from the kennels and Hannibal needs to burn off some energy. There's no break in the chicken wire, so we could come with you now."

Patricia gave Clair the empty basket and a hug. "See you tomorrow. Have a good rest of the day."

She led the way up the path with Sophie. Picking a stalk of lavender from a bush, Patricia crushed it to release the calming perfume. Behind them, Rocky the Rooster roused his feathers and crowed triumphantly at their departure.

Chapter 3

As Patricia and Anthony came through the arched door in the wall, from Stables Cottage onto the main track, four ponies with student riders and helpers came back from Potlatch Wood. There was the clip-clop of hooves on the cobbles and a creak of saddle leather as youngsters called to Sophie, and Patricia waved to volunteers. She turned to Anthony, "Clair likes the students to be out as much as possible before the winter weather closes in."

There were several disability vans in the parking lot, their drivers awaiting children going home. To one side stood a white 4 x 4 sports vehicle with its windows a quarter open. A large, wire dog crate filled the rear and Patricia could see Hannibal pacing inside. She puzzled. Had she seen this vehicle before? Anthony opened the passenger door and brought out a pair of black gumboots. "This was in one of the garages at the Manor House. It belongs to my sister but is just the right size for Hannibal's crate. I have borrowed it and she can drive my Mercedes if she comes back. Do you still have your Morris 1000?"

"I do! My son Paul bought it for me for my sixtieth birthday and it is special, as I learned how to drive in one just like it. My father was an engineer in the Cowley plant where it was built."

Sports shoes off and gumboots on, Anthony pulled on a waterproof shooting jacket and leather hat. "Morris 1000's are collector's items these days."

Patricia smiled ruefully. "They are, if they are in pristine condition. I do not have a garage and my car must park in St. Peter's parking lot. It has rust, but I love its original sage-green paintwork, the leather bucket seats, and rosewood trim. The engine is good, so I shall keep it until it finally falls apart!"

Anthony studied his reflection in the side mirror of the 4 x 4 and angled the leather hat to a jaunty angle. He caught the slight upward movement of Patricia's lips and struck a pose, grinning. "What? I know it is vanity but I have so little hair and this will stop raindrops from falling on my head."

"You look dashing, like an Australian stockman."

Hannibal yelped and Anthony opened the hatchback door. He carefully attached the leash to Hannibal's harness before opening the crate. Even so, Hannibal leaped from the tailgate to say hi to Sophie and almost pulled Anthony's arm from its socket.

Patricia hurried down the path into the wood, so that Hannibal would follow Sophie. Anthony clicked his remote to close the windows and lock the doors, then he and Hannibal caught up with them.

Rooks called from the bare branches above them and Anthony looked up. "I never played here as a kid, as I was away at boarding school, so I do not know Potlatch Wood. But most of Summerfield seems unchanged compared to London."

Hannibal charged off after a fascinating smell and dragged Anthony after him. When they got back, Anthony was breathless and Patricia asked, "Why have you decided to return now?"

"I intended to retire before this, but the business is addictive. Once I had Hannibal, it seemed time to relocate.

I can go to London for Board Meetings. I enjoy making things happen and am worried about all the spare time I'm going to have."

Hannibal stopped in a bush and they all stopped.

"I am sure that once you are settled in Summerfield, lots of opportunities will come along. Have you seen these inertia reel leashes?" Patricia held up the blue handle of Sophie's. "They let the dog run a certain distance and then you can bring them back in again."

She pressed the button and allowed Sophie to go to Hannibal, then pressed it again to bring her back. "Try it with Hannibal."

They transferred leashes and Anthony let Hannibal out on a long line, whereupon he bounced on Sophie and knocked her off her feet. She got up with a disgusted look at him and Anthony reeled Hannibal in like a trout on a fishing line. "Sorry."

From then on, he worked to manage Hannibal better and they walked along the track in a more civilized way. Hannibal explored the undergrowth and Anthony then brought him back. "That's better! I always wanted a dog when I was a kid, but it was not possible."

Patricia warmed to him, "My late husband was allergic to animal hair so we could not have a dog. When I moved to Summerfield, I found Sophie at the Rescue Center and it was love at first sight. We go everywhere together."

"She's lovely but I don't know the breed."

"The Irish setters are red, but Sophie is an English setter, white with black markings. Her first owners lived in an apartment where dogs were not allowed. They wanted a puppy, so they dripped bleach into her drinking water to burn her vocal cords, which prevents her from barking."

Anthony looked horrified. "How could anyone do something like that?"

Patricia felt drawn to him again. "They were reported

and prosecuted, but the bleach worked. Sophie cannot bark."

She stopped. "I am being a dog bore."

Anthony was practicing with Hannibal and the leash. "I am rapidly becoming one as well! Go on, please."

Patricia smiled at him, "The other thing about Sophie is that I can rarely let her off the leash. Something spooked her, and she ran almost to the county line before someone caught her. Luckily, she is micro-chipped, and the police brought her back. I only let her off the leash in safe places now, because if she's scared, she can run so fast."

Hannibal walked quietly next to Anthony and Patricia chuckled, "You probably gather that I think Sophie is perfect. She is, except for a tendency to drool anywhere near food, which is revolting."

"Ah, we don't have a drooling problem, but I needed to move Hannibal's bed outside my room. He snores so loudly that I cannot get to sleep!"

Patricia was watching the black dog. "He is crossbred. but did the military authorities tell you anything about his background?"

Anthony nodded. "Sniffer dogs are normally Labradors or German Shepherds, but someone gave them Hannibal because of his extraordinary ability to scent. Canine beauty did not matter in Afghanistan, so he was trained and sent there. The black coat, square body, and broad head is Rottweiler and the rest of him is German shepherd."

Patricia ignored the scars and bomb-mangled ears. "He has beautiful eyes."

Anthony hesitated, as if deciding whether to tell her something. "The reason I brought him to Summerfield now is that he has PTSD, post-traumatic stress disorder. He cries if he is alone and cowers into the ground if something noisy like a tractor goes past. He is not confident about anything."

Patricia felt hurt for a dog who had saved countless lives.

Anthony went on, "Hannibal warned David of the explosion before it blew. David had counseling for PTSD. The kennels staff told me I should have Hannibal put out of his misery if I could not take him home and try to help him."

They had reached the path leading to the village. Patricia took Sophie's collar and held out the short leash to a kind man with an ugly dog. "I admire you for giving him a second chance."

Anthony took the short leash, attached it, and gave the extended one back to Patricia. "Thank you for letting me try that. Might you have some time to walk with us and help me train him?"

"I would be glad to help but you must also take him to a training class. He needs to meet other dogs and learn to obey so that he can trust you."

"I will go online and look for a class and buy him an extending leash tomorrow. When are you free for another walk? We will do much better with you and Sophie to coach us."

Patricia thought for a moment. "I am busy tomorrow and have tenants moving into my rental cottage on Saturday morning, but I'm free in the afternoon."

They exchanged phone numbers and Patricia walked home. "I'm sorry you got bounced on, Sophie. We will stop Hannibal from doing that. But how lovely to have new friends to walk with! Getting to know Anthony better will be fun!"

Chapter 4

The following morning Patricia drove her Morris 1000 through Summerfield village. She turned left after the War Memorial down Stables Lane. It was narrow and originally a cart track. Over the years, wheels had cut a deep lane with high banks on either side. With disability vans driving up and down, Clair had wanted to widen it. But she did not own the land to either side and could only raise enough money to cut turnouts for passing. As she drove, Patricia opened her window to listen for oncoming traffic. Sophie leaned over her shoulder, her soft ears flapping in the frosty air.

Halfway down, Patricia heard the clip-clop of hooves and pulled into a turnout. Around the corner came two magnificent black Friesian horses, pulling a long cart, driven by her friend Robert. Patricia jumped out of the car and closed the door quickly, to stop an eager Sophie from following. She had taken off her red coat to drive. In blue jeans and a grey, turtleneck sweater, Patricia crossed her arms to keep warm while she waited.

Robert Kennett was Clair's Yard Manager. He grinned down at Patricia from the box seat high on the cart and brought the horses to a halt beside her. "Good morning, welcome back!"

Robert was in his fifties and had been an officer in the Mounted Police. An accident forced early retirement and Patricia had become a friend when she ran the Stables office. Like many of the staff, Robert was passionate about horses and kids, but not administration! Patricia had helped him with paperwork. He had also gone through a sticky divorce and she had been there for him. Patricia was pleased to see him now. "A good morning to you too! I have never seen Blackbird and Rebel in harness before. What are you up to with these guys?"

Robert was a big man with broad shoulders, a rugged face, and greying hair in a buzz cut. He suffered back pain from his accident and now Patricia saw him lean forward on the bench, easing his shoulders. "Ted bought them from a man who gave up competitive driving, because they could also be ridden. A friend of mine owns the funeral company in Banbury and found a Victorian hearse. He asked me to train these two to pull it for special funerals."

Patricia missed their chats now that she worked at St. Peter's. Robert had seen much of life and brought that maturity to work with youngsters and volunteers. A loss for the police was a gain for Summerfield Stables.

A pigeon flew low over the horses and both tossed their heads, jingling their harness. Robert adjusted his double reins and saluted her with his coaching whip. "We need to get on. Hope to see you later. Walk on, boys."

Patricia watched as he maneuvered the cart around the next bend, then jumped back into the car and drove on.

* * *

At Stables Cottage, Jossie came skidding across the stone tiles to welcome them. He was a six-year-old pedigree Springer spaniel and his tail wagged so hard it whipped his brown-and-white body from side to side!

"Hi Ted, it's only me. I'll be there in a minute with tea."

Patricia had firmly latched the arched gate to the stables yard when she came in. She let Sophie and Jossie out to play, switched on the kettle, and looked around while she waited for it to boil. Clair and David had been married for six months and she had not seen their remodeling of Stables Cottage. The kitchen/family room was newly painted, and a lovely new couch stood next to the coffee table. She was glad to see they had kept the old copper pans shining above the stove and Grandma May's hand-embroidered cushions were still in their place of honor.

Gathering the tea things onto a tray, Patricia carried them to Ted's room. It was on the far side of the family room, overlooking the orchard. Ted was not in his usual chair by the window but sat up on a new hospital bed, leaning against the angled back rest. He was watching soccer on TV and muted the sound. "Hello, Patricia. Look at this marvelous bed! David bought it for the Manor House when he came out of the hospital and now I have it."

He demonstrated the remote controls. "Up, down, backrest angled or flat. I breathe better at night if I can sit up to sleep."

Patricia put the tea tray on a low table. "Great! Well done, David."

Ted leaned forward to look in the tea cup she handed him. His thatch of white hair caught the light, neatly brushed to one side, as always. "You remembered. I only have half a cup these days, my wrists can't hold a full one anymore."

Ted was dressed in comfortable grey sweatpants with a red plaid shirt. Alpine slipper socks encased his feet, which stuck out from under a crocheted throw across his legs. Patricia sat down in the armchair next to his bed. They drank tea and watched silent figures running around on the screen. Ted turned the TV off. "I saw you and Sophie in the orchard yesterday, but I was too upset to come and speak to you. That Hannibal is not here, is he?"

Patricia shook her head. "Anthony understands about the hens now. He never owned a dog before."

Ted snorted. "Then why does he have a traumatized animal like that? No eggs this morning, like I said."

Patricia tried to smooth things over. "Clair said your hens were okay. Hannibal served his country, like David did. Without Anthony, Hannibal would have been euthanized."

Ted was an old countryman and well-used to the death of animals in his care. "Pure sentimentality! That was a working dog, serving with the army in Afghanistan. He should have stayed there."

He was getting upset and stopped to breathe, inhaling sharply. The skin on his neck was paper-thin and blue veins stood out on his forehead. Patricia drank her tea quietly and a few minutes later, Ted asked quietly, "Do you believe in Heaven?"

Patricia thought for a few moments. Ted's outburst about Anthony and the dog were a cover for his anxiety. "I do. I respect all faiths, but I worship God through His Son, Jesus Christ. I believe that God reunites us with our loved ones in Heaven."

Ted plucked at the crocheted throw. "What if I don't make it? I haven't been good, like May always was."

Patricia leaned back, her mug in both hands. "I wish I'd known May, but I do know the many kinds things you have done. When it is your time, I think May will be standing waiting with St. Peter, to welcome you inside the pearly gates."

Ted's eyes lit up in a crinkly smile. "You are kind. It is nice that you think so."

Patricia took his cup and put it back on the tray. "Would you like Tim Fell to call and see you? He is a sympathetic man and knows the Scriptures."

Ted shook his head. "He did a nice wedding ceremony for Clair and David, but I don't know him. Might you come and read some of the Bible to me, like May did? I'd like that."

"I'd like that too, but I am worried about your breathing. Would you let me drive you to the doctor?"

Ted roared with laughter, which made him wheeze. "I know who put you up to that!"

He recovered. "I know what they'll tell me. My heart is wearing out and I just need to put up with it. Clair fusses too much."

"She loves you and you have not seen the doctor since January. If you let me take you, she won't worry anymore."

"Maybe you are right. I don't like to make her anxious."

Patricia accessed Banbury Medical Center on the laptop from her bag. "Next available appointment is Tuesday at noon. I will book it and check with Clair."

Ted looked astonished. "Is that it? You didn't even speak to a Receptionist."

Patricia laughed. "They do not have Receptionists anymore. It's all on the automated system now."

"The wonders of modern science." Ted clicked on the TV. "Could you let Jossie in and close the curtains before you go? The cricket is just starting, England versus Australia. Should be a good match."

She did as he asked. "Stay well and I'll see you Tuesday."

* * *

Patricia and Sophie crossed the stable yard and into the Reception area. It was on familiar territory and smelled of horses, hay, and saddle soap, as opposed to damp and mold at St. Peter's. A countertop separated the open area from the office and Patricia called, "Anybody here?"

The smiling face of Audrey Partridge appeared around the screen divider. "Come in! Clair said you would look at the computer with me. Thank goodness! The legal stuff is complex, and I keep losing files."

Patricia went through the side door and Sophie lay down in her usual place under the office table.

Audrey was about the same height as Patricia but a little older She sat on an office swivel chair, rounded and comfortable in a rose-pink skirt and knitted cardigan. Her flyaway hair had once been auburn but was now mixed with grey. She had clipped it back into the nape of her neck, but wisps escaped around her face. Patricia pulled up a chair next to the computer. They knew each other well from St. Mary's where Audrey played the organ on Sundays and the piano for choir practices.

Patricia found the file. People who volunteer with children and vulnerable adults go through police screening and the database needed regular updating. She took Audrey through each step of the process and waited quietly while she completed it.

Through the window to the indoor arena, she could see Clair and David working with a young man on Winston, Robert's horse. On either side of him walked a volunteer. Clair was the qualified Instructor for *Riding with Challenges;* David was on the two-year training course with the Head Office in London. They were both dressed in black riding pants with blue Summerfield Stables fleece jackets.

Audrey finished her inputting and followed Patricia's gaze. "Did you hear that Anthony Bartlett-Brown has moved back to the Manor House?"

"Yes, I met him with Clair."

Anthony's part in the drama of the lease to Summerfield Stables was unknown outside the management team. He had raised a substantial loan for David to bid at the auction. He loaned him another million from the business that secured the lease for Clair and David and their future together.

"Oh my," Audrey looked back at the computer screen, "what have I done now?"

Patricia sorted it and Sophie popped out from under the desk to greet Clair. "Hi everyone!" She bent to pat Sophie. "Patricia, in all the drama yesterday, I did not even ask if your renovations were complete."

"The painting was completed while I was in Oxford, and my tenants move in tomorrow morning."

Audrey swiveled on her chair to face them and her voice was wistful. "When we were at elementary school, my best friend lived in Number 1, Halfmoon Cottages. She had six brothers and sisters. I would love to see that cottage modernized."

"You are most welcome to come before the tenants move in." Patricia glanced at her watch. "Would you care to come with me now? I need to head back as my winter firewood logs are being delivered."

Audrey looked at Clair. "Could I go with Patricia and make up the time on Monday?"

"Of course! I have a basket of apples for Patricia. I'll carry it to her car while you shut down the computer."

Clair picked up the basket she had left on the shelf in Reception, and they walked to the parking lot. "How did it go with Granddad?"

"All good. He appreciated that you were worried, and we have a doctor's appointment on Tuesday."

"Thank you, that is one weight off my mind." Sophie jumped into the back seat of the car as Clair put the basket of windfall apples into the trunk. Clair still seemed preoccupied and Patricia asked, "What's up? You are still not your usual cheery self."

Clair leaned against the car. "You are the most confidential person in the world, and I know it will not go any further."

Audrey came out of Reception and hurried toward them, pulling on her coat.

"David and I are so happy together, but we have a medical problem too. We want to start a family, but nothing is happening. We went to the Oxford clinic and my tests are okay. David needs to see a specialist. They think it may be his blast injuries from Afghanistan."

Chapter 5

Clair assumed her normal cheerful voice as Audrey approached. "Okay. I am off to eat lunch with Granddad. Enjoy the cottages and I'll see you on Monday."

Audrey settled into the passenger seat of the Morris and fastened her seatbelt. She turned to pat Sophie, who was lying on her blanket in the back. "I am looking forward to rehearsing our Christmas program at choir tonight."

The Morris chugged up the hill and Patricia remembered something she had been meaning to ask Audrey. "You have lived in Summerfield all your life; do you know where the name, Halfmoon Cottages, comes from?"

Audrey laughed. "Quirky village names just happen, don't they? Maybe the name comes from that clearing beside St. Peter's, which is a wonderful place to see the moon. I live in Catbrain Lane, and no one knows where that comes from either!"

At the top of Stables Lane, Patricia stopped to look left and right before pulling out. Audrey *tut-tutted* and pointed at the War Memorial, "Look at those kids, they should be in school."

Mounted on a set of steps, a tall stone cross bore the names of Summerfield people who died in two World Wars.

A group of teenagers lounged on the steps, and some were smoking.

"Perhaps they missed the bus."

Audrey was skeptical. "I know them, and they missed it on purpose. Still, I should not criticize, we used to miss the bus too, when I was in school."

Patricia continued along Summerfield's one long street between lovely thatched cottages to the pub, the Potlatch Inn. "I love these cottages but couldn't afford to buy one when I came to Summerfield. Number 7 looked fabulous last Christmas. They had so many lights on the cottage that it brightened the entire village. I loved the sleigh and reindeer along the ridge of the roof."

Audrey turned to look at the cottage as they passed. "The lights were up by this time last year, but I heard he lost his job. His wife is a stay-at-home mum with two little ones, and they are struggling. Maybe we could put together a Christmas gift basket for them?"

Audrey helped Patricia collect Food Bank donations for needy families. They stored them in plastic bins in the robing room of St. Peter's and had a list to prepare for a special Christmas delivery.

"Great idea."

Patricia parked in front of St. Peter's and took the basket of apples from the trunk. Audrey held Sophie on her leash, and they walked for three minutes along Church Lane to the cottages. They rounded the bend by the gigantic oak tree and Audrey exclaimed, "Oh my! They look so different from the last time I saw them!"

Halfmoon Cottages were two separate homes, but from a distance looked like a kid's drawing of one little house. There was a central chimney between two sides that were mirror images in Victorian brick. The roof was of potlatch slates, cleaned of moss and lichen. The cottages had identical windows, two up and two down, on either side of identical pale blue front doors. Paling fences enclosing each front yard were painted the same color.

Patricia smiled as she viewed her year's work. "The Sales flyer said *Victorian semi-detached cottages, built in 1890, in need of renovation and TLC.* They certainly needed tender loving care, and most of my pension savings have gone as well! They are finished and I enjoyed making them look beautiful."

Audrey gazed up at the roof as Patricia opened the gate of Number 2. "My house is in the Council complex at the other end of the village and I have not been down this lane for years. People said these cottages did not sell because they had no garage or parking. They were empty for a long time."

Off leash, Sophie dashed around the side of Number 2 to the backyard as Patricia opened the front door. The hallway smelled of fresh paint and Patricia turned to the right, "This is the sitting room, which opens into the kitchen and family room, through these bi-fold doors."

They walked through to a spacious area, bright with four skylight windows. "I had this sunroom extension built across both cottages. It has the laundry and a shower room and opens onto the deck."

Through the glass back door, they could see Sophie snuffling around the back gate at the bottom of the yard. A six-foot trellis fence stood between the deck of Number 2 and Patricia's deck next door. Halfway down the path, the fence dropped to three feet for the rest of the way to the gate. "I had the fence put in for greater privacy."

Patricia switched on the kitchen lights and the room came to life. The walls were a deep, chalky white and a wide oak beam arched across the ceiling. In the middle was a large cooking island with double sinks and pale grey cupboards on all sides.

Above the granite worktop hung four lights on long

cords with domed metal shades, like in a Victorian railway station. The floor tiles were soft grey, and they had painted the central heating pipes the same color as a feature against the white. Audrey's voice was wistful. "It is beautiful. Your tenants will love it."

Patricia was pleased. "Thank you. Come next door and see my cottage, which is furnished."

She called Sophie, and they went out of Number 2 and in at the gate of Number 1. A robin hopped across the small lawn and Sophie gave chase. It flew into the oak tree and scolded her. Inside the front door, Patricia turned left this time and led Audrey into her sitting room.

A comfy sofa stood opposite the small fireplace, which was laid ready to light the fire. There was a flat-screen TV on a low unit, surrounded by family photographs, and a hard-wearing beige carpet covered the floor. The cottage was warm with central heating, with books, ornaments, and plants on the windowsills.

"This is so cozy." Audrey followed Patricia up the staircase, which had a white wooden handrail and the same carpet. The landing window had a pleasant reading alcove with an upholstered bench seat. "I like to sit here in the afternoons when the winter sun shines in and I can see Sophie in the backyard."

Patricia's bedroom was feminine, with white furniture and lilac floral curtains. The main bathroom was next to it and opposite the second bedroom. "The builder had a job to get a bathtub in here! We managed by using a three-quarter size with a shower over it."

Patricia paused to look in at twin beds and contemporary furnishings in the second bedroom. "I hope my granddaughters might come and stay with me at some point."

Audrey bent to look out of the small window. "You don't find it spooky, so near to St. Peter's graveyard?"

Patricia looked surprised. "I have never thought about

that! I love the quiet and the owls calling from Potlatch Wood."

She was about to lead back downstairs when she spotted a truck on the track at the back of the cottages. It was towing a trailer of logs. "I am so sorry, Audrey. I was going to make tea, but I need to get my logs into the old pigsty before it rains."

She opened the window and called, "Hello! I am just coming down. Please, could you unload them there?" She pointed to the pigsty.

Audrey laughed as they went down the stairs. "All this modernization, and you kept the pigsty?"

"It does seem odd, but I have no room for logs up by the cottages. The pigsty is deep and dry, with no evidence of pigs. It will make a perfect woodstore!"

Audrey collected her bag from the kitchen. "Thanks so much for showing me around. I think you have done an outstanding job."

Patricia waved as she shut the gate. "See you later."

She hurried to pull on an old rain jacket and thick gardening gloves, glancing at the dark clouds massing over St. Peter's. By the time she reached the bottom of the yard, the driver had unloaded the logs and left.

The logs were heavy. She had to use two hands to throw each one into the back of the pigsty. Sophie sat and watched her but suddenly, jumped up and ran toward the house. Patricia looked around and saw her son striding down the path. He looked so like his father that she dropped the log and hurried toward him. "Paul! Is something wrong? Why didn't you call?"

Chapter 6

Paul Anderson, Patricia's only child, bent from his six-foot frame to give her a hug. "Mum, I called you! There is a message on your mobile phone, which is probably on the kitchen counter. It says, *In Banbury, coming to see you on the way home.*

Patricia glanced over his shoulder and he noticed her disappointment as he stroked Sophie's head. "The girls are at their ballet class."

"Never mind," Patricia smiled up at him. "You are here."

She looked up at heavy clouds moving in on the wind. "Would you help me get these logs into the pigsty? Then we could have a big catch-up."

Paul held out his hand for the gloves. "You sit down for a minute and I will do it for you."

"Thank you, dear."

Paul was forty-four years old, born ten months after she married Ron. They had not intended to start a family so quickly, but Patricia fell in love with her baby boy as soon as they placed him in her arms. She and Ron could not have been happier. But two years later, for no apparent reason, the next baby was stillborn, and Patricia became sick with postnatal depression. Ron had been supportive. "Get well again and other babies will come along."

Patricia thought that today there would be many more tests and treatments. But then, there was nothing, and more babies had not come along, so Paul was especially precious.

She sat on the low wall watching him effortlessly throwing logs into the pigsty. "I can't keep up with all your work travel. Where have you been?"

"I got back last night from Shenzhen, China, and passed out with exhaustion."

Patricia looked at him sharply. She had heard about this 'exhaustion' before and worried he was drinking too much. Paul had been good at foreign languages in high school and gone on to do a business degree, with Mandarin. He started a high-tech solutions business with two friends from the university. Patricia did not really understand what their business did, but nodded sagely, when he talked about it.

Paul was a handsome man, with the same grey eyes and thick black hair as Ron's. She smiled, remembering them going to the barber together. They both hated it if it got long and wavy. Paul dressed formally for his business, but today wore old jeans and a faded football shirt as his way of signaling that he was not working. "I woke to the usual family Friday. Eve had taken the girls to school and there were four messages on my phone with chores I needed to do."

He sighed, seized a log in each hand and threw them into the woodstore. "I have collected stuff from Banbury. After seeing you, I pick up Charlotte and Amber from class and take them to a friend's house. I need to be back to escort Eve to a Music Society Fundraiser, when I would rather relax and watch the game on TV."

Patricia found other gloves inside the pigsty. "I will help finish the logs. How are the girls? I enjoyed seeing them when I was in Oxford, but they don't want to come here."

Paul laughed. "They are teenagers. They have little time for Eve and me, let alone anyone else. It is unbelievable that

Charlotte will be sixteen in March."

The logs were almost all inside and Patricia fetched the yard broom. "I know the girls want to be with their friends, but I miss the things we did together when they were young."

Paul took the broom and swept up woodchips. "Are you okay here, Mum? Sometimes I worry about you."

Patricia smiled. "That's lovely, dear, but I'm fine. I have Sophie and my project at St. Peter's. The tenants are coming tomorrow and maybe they will become new friends."

"We thought you would stay in Oxford when you retired, slow down a bit, and maybe marry again?"

Patricia stiffened. "I have no intention of slowing down, nor marrying again, thank you."

Paul laid the gloves on the wall. Abruptly, he said, "Eve is upset because you won't come to look after the girls. It's only for three days, while she is on her creative arts course. You did it last year."

Eve, Paul's wife, was a petite blonde with blue eyes. They had met at college, where she studied music and played violin professionally. She had stopped playing, and taught music when Charlotte was born, but became a stay-at-home mum when Amber came along. Her life was always busy, but it was largely with homemaking and organizing activities for the girls. She wanted a new career, but Paul was away such a lot.

Patricia pulled her jacket tighter around her. "Is that the real reason you are here? Eve told you to round up your mum and get her back to the grindstone?"

The storm clouds were almost overhead. Paul stuck his hands in his front pockets. "Not told, I was asked. Eve needs a break and the girls are sad you will not come."

Patricia was indignant. "That is not true! I saw them recently. Eve only calls me in her honey tones when she wants me to do something. I have a new job and a life here. I can't come this time."

Paul's voice was low, "Or ever? Eve thinks you could do it if you wanted to. Would you come this once, Mum? For me?"

Patricia looked down at the concrete and her cheeks felt hot. "I am deliberately not coming. For you."

"What do you mean?"

Exasperated, she looked directly at him. "The last time I looked after the girls for three days, Eve returned positively radiant."

Paul shrugged. "She enjoys getting together with old friends."

Patricia said nothing. He took his hands from his pockets and stood up straight. "Are you suggesting she is having an affair?"

"I am suggesting that you are away too much. I am uncomfortable covering for her overnight when you are out of the country."

Paul's face was red. "The business does not run itself, you know."

"One day you may come back from China and they will have changed the locks on your beautiful house. Served with divorce papers, you will end up in a one-bedroom apartment, paying for everything but only seeing the girls every second weekend."

Heavy raindrops began to splash on the roof of the pigsty. Paul stormed up the path and shouted over his shoulder, "Eve says you are getting bitter in your old age, and I agree with her!"

Patricia did not feel the downpour, only a pain in her stomach that doubled her over. Sophie nudged her with a worried wet nose. "I said too much again. Do people ever forgive you if you tell them the truth?"

The rain plastered white hair to her head. In slow motion, she loaded a few logs into the yard cart and trundled it up the path. In the kitchen, her mobile phone winked with the message from her son.

"They will probably not even ask me for Christmas lunch this year."

* * *

Luckily, there was no more time to brood. Patricia toweled Sophie dry and fed her. After a quick shower, a change of clothes, and a microwaved meal, Patricia hurried along Church Lane to meet Sarah.

Climbing into the silver Mini Cooper, Patricia stowed her purse behind the passenger seat. "If we have any more rain, I swear, I will grow webbed feet!"

Sarah smiled, "Great weather for ducks!"

Sarah Jessop was the housekeeper at the Manor House. She was in her fifties and taller than Patricia, with grey hair smoothed into a neat roll at the back of her head and held with a clip. She was wearing a brown raincoat, with beige slacks, an orange blouse, and a silk scarf in swirls of orange around her neck.

They took turns driving to church and choir practice. The Morris 1000 said a lot about Patricia, and Sarah said, "Driving the Mini liberates me. I have been in domestic service all my working life. But I am more than a housekeeper, and retirement is not far away."

Riding in Sarah's car, Patricia felt too close to the road and she held the handle above her seat. "How is it going with Anthony back?"

Sarah zoomed around a corner, the brilliant headlights lighting up hedgerows. "It is delightful! When David married Clair, I was worried he might shut the Manor House and I would lose my job. But Anthony and Hannibal have settled in and keep me busy. Am I right in thinking that your tenants move in tomorrow? Are they people you know from Oxford?"

Patricia was surprised. "I told you. I put an ad in the *Oxford Church Times* when I was on my verger's course."

"No, you did not tell me that."

Patricia's brow wrinkled. "I'm sorry, I thought I did. There was so much going on. Anyway, I had a few replies. One was an author, a male, but the cottages are so isolated that I decided a female would be better. A woman applied with a daughter who has a four-month-old baby. The finance and references checked out okay and I got the impression they were fleeing an abusive relationship. I did something socially useful and offered them the cottage."

Sarah parked the Mini next to St. Mary's church. Lights shone through stained-glass windows and colored the puddles. Sarah held the door open for Patricia. "You are handling everything yourself? Not using a rental agency?"

Patricia held the church door for Sarah to follow her in. Audrey was playing the piano and they could hear the murmur of voices. "The fees were horrendous, and I need to watch every penny now. I got a standard Tenancy Agreement from an online legal website, and we signed it with witnesses."

Sarah frowned, "I hope it works out okay. You are sometimes a bit of a do-gooder."

* * *

Choir practice was fine, but the drive home was largely silent. Patricia intended to walk Sophie and watch TV by her fire, but she felt drained.

Sophie welcomed her joyfully. "We will do a quick walk around St. Peter's and have an early night. Busy day tomorrow!"

Sophie ran ahead on her long leash, and Patricia wondered about Sarah's words. She thought she was trying to be a good Christian by offering somewhere safe to two women who needed help. But *do-gooder* did not sound like a compliment.

The rain had blown away and a crescent moon rode high above the clearing. Patricia loved living away from the noise of the city. She and Sophie went their normal circular route—along Church Lane, in through the front gate, along the path by the back of the building, and out the back gate to the cottages. Patricia had a flashlight and there was a streetlamp on the corner.

Back in her cottage, Patricia locked the doors and switched off the lights. Climbing the stairs to her room, she knelt at the open window and sent love to her family and to all the world. Her mother said the same words to her that she had said to Paul, and then to her granddaughters, "Goodnight, God bless, see you in the morning."

Sophie was in her bed on the floor next to her. Patricia had just snuggled down under the quilt when her phone *pinged* with a text. Patricia snaked an arm out into the cold to grab it.

Looking forward to walking tomorrow. Meet at the path by your cottages? Please confirm time.
   Anthony

Chapter 7

Happy Saturday! Patricia slept for eight hours and woke to bright sunshine pouring in through the bedroom window. The sky was a frosty, bright blue, and the weather forecast promised no rain for at least twenty-four hours. The city mutes weather patterns but Patricia found the changeable seasons a joy of living in the countryside.

She let Sophie into the backyard and showered in the downstairs bathroom. In a comfortable, baggy sweater with blue jeans, she sang along to the radio as she mixed a batch of cookie dough. Amber, her youngest granddaughter, loved to cook, and they had made this recipe together. Adding a scoop of chocolate chips, she cut the rounds, laid them on baking trays and popped them into the oven. "Time for a last check."

Patricia grabbed the keys for Number 2 from the hook and pulled on her boots. Everything looked beautiful next door, and she left a little card on the countertop.

Welcome! I hope you will be happy in your new home.
Patricia

Back in her cottage, she brought Sophie in from the yard. "Today, we will have a proper breakfast, sitting at the table!"

Many mornings, wearing paint-splattered dungarees and a headscarf, she had grabbed a bowl of cereal before putting innumerable coats of paint onto new plaster. Sophie ate a balanced doggy breakfast while Patricia sat down to scrambled eggs with toast and coffee. She loved to work hard and it pleased her that the cottage next door had tenants arriving today and would earn its keep. Patricia was ready to focus on St. Peter's.

Sipping coffee from a favorite mug, Patricia watched a young robin with a bright scarlet breast hop onto the patio table. He flew down on the other side of the glass and Sophie leaped. He flew away with a flutter of wings and Patricia leaned down to turn Sophie's nose away from the glass. "He is just a baby. He will not survive the winter if you scare him away from the food."

The timer pinged and Patricia opened the oven with padded gloves. The cookies were crispy, golden perfection and Patricia spread them to cool on a wire rack. She gave her last corner of toast to Sophie and was loading the dishwasher when an old black car pulled up outside. Her new tenant, Donna Smithers, was in the driver's seat. Her daughter, Tracey, and the baby sat in the back.

They had met to view the cottage several weeks before when Patricia was on the verger's course in Oxford. Donna and she had met again to sign the tenancy agreement. Patricia had hoped to get to know them more before they moved in, but Donna said it was not possible. They were saving money and needed to stay with friends in London until the cottage was ready.

Patricia put on her quilted coat and with Sophie at her heels went out to greet her tenants. "Good morning, you have a beautiful day for moving in."

Donna was lifting a baby stroller from the trunk of the car. "Good morning."

She carried it to the path next to Patricia. Donna was an inch or so taller than Patricia and had blond hair pulled into a tight bun on top of her head. She wore the same outfit she had worn on the other two occasions they had met. But the baby stroller was brand new, and Patricia realized that she would spend money on her grandchild first. Tracey had seemed nervous when they first met, but she was different today. Under a denim jacket, her white T-shirt fit tightly across her chest and she wore slim-fit jeans with slashes below both knees. Her hair was spiked with gel and she had strongly defined, black eyebrows. Lifting the sleeping baby from the car, she laid him in the stroller. He had on a little blue snowsuit and Patricia smiled. "What a good baby!"

Tracey gave her a half smile and Patricia turned to hand the folder to Donna. "Thank you for setting up the monthly payment and here are your two sets of keys. This folder has information on things like recycling and trash collection."

"We are grateful for your kindness. A friend is following with our things."

Donna spoke stiffly and seemed unwilling to chat, which contrasted with her enthusiasm when they came to view the cottage. Perhaps they had a disturbed night with the baby. Patricia remembered Paul teething and how groggy she felt with poor sleep. Sophie had not come close and Patricia thought she should introduce her. "This is Sophie, she is very gentle."

Neither woman smiled, nor moved to pat her. Yet Donna had said they liked dogs.

"I am going to the market now. But just to mention again, this space is for loading and unloading only. We have permission to use St. Peter's parking lot, so the car needs to park there when you have finished."

Back home, Patricia put the cookies into an airtight box to take around after her walk with Anthony. Pulling on her white hat and mittens, she looked in the long mirror and laughed at the reflection. "Oh dear, Sophie! I look like Mrs. Christmas again."

Summerfield's market stalls stood on the sidewalks and paved square, but everyone wore boots. She headed up Church Lane, one hand holding Sophie's leash, the other towing a black-and-white-checked shopping cart. Every week she filled it with local goodies.

St. Peter's churchyard was zebra-striped with sunshine and shade. Patricia walked past the yew trees and table tombs slumped among the brambles. Headstones leaned at crazy angles in the long grass and she stopped for a minute, focused on a patch by the wall. Rounding the corner of the church, she spotted Jim Lawrence cutting grass at the far end of the Memorial Garden. He shut off the mower and came over. "Good morning, off to the market?"

It was obvious that she was, but Patricia nodded and smiled pleasantly. Jim was about five feet, eight inches tall with a slight stoop. He had a long face and a grey ponytail. His main job was as Summerfield's only taxi driver. It was irregular work, so he was also the general handyman for St. Peter's. He wore very nice casuals for driving, but today, an old brown coverall bulged with sweaters underneath, to keep out the cold.

Jim was a friend of Ted's. He was in his late fifties, younger than Ted, but both their wives had been in the Oxford hospital. Jim's wife had died just after May and they still got together regularly.

"Couldn't do a thing in all that rain, so I'm cutting the grass now."

"I wanted to ask, are there Christmas roses at the back of the church? They are one of my favorites."

Jim blew on reddened hands and nodded. "They are in bud right now. We get snowdrops in January, and daffodils and bluebells after that. No one visits those graves, so I leave the undergrowth and don't disturb the flowers."

An enticing smell of fresh bread and hot coffee wafted past, and Patricia sniffed appreciatively. Jim waved a hand and set off back to his mower. "I'll get back to work, see you later."

Patricia and Sophie went through the front gate of St. Peter's, into the bustle of people and market stalls.

* * *

The organizers of Summerfield market closed the road to vehicles on Saturday and erected booths. Identical red-and-white-striped awnings covered the tops and sides. But inside there were many different vendors of vegetables and meat, dairy products, eggs, baked goods, and crafts. Patricia thought that shopping must have been like this in medieval times. Everyone was wearing hats and gloves in the chilly sunshine. She wandered the stalls with Sophie, greeting many people she knew from working at the Stables.

Consulting her list, Patricia bought potatoes, carrots, and a cauliflower from her usual vegetable stall. She had apples from Clair to make applesauce, so she picked up a leg of pork from the butcher for a Sunday roast, and a bag of marrow bones for Sophie. The Potlatch Inn was selling hot dogs and the aroma had pulled a line of hungry kids beneath its unusual pub sign.

It was a large wooden sign painted with a grey boulder standing in a green field, with darker hills and woods behind. A geologist from Oxford University had found that Potlatch Wood was on the end of a melted glacier. A potlatch was the local name for a glacial rock, smoothed by the moving ice. Over the centuries, villagers collected them, to split and use as roofing tiles. Halfmoon Cottages had a Victorian potlatch roof.

Patricia glanced at her watch and headed home. She was

pleased to see Donna's car in St. Peter's parking lot, but a large white van with a trailer stood in front of the cottages. It entirely filled the space. But there was no one in sight as she and Sophie squeezed past.

Patricia ate a quick sandwich while she put groceries away and filled a thermos flask with hot tea. She put it into her backpack with two mugs and a small box of cookies. Adding a bottle of water for the dogs, Patricia changed into her walking boots for mud and locked the back door. Walking down the back path with Sophie, she resisted the temptation to look back as she latched the gate behind them and hurried to meet Anthony.

Chapter 8

At the entrance to Potlatch Wood, Hannibal sat alert by Anthony's side and Patricia could see the blue handle of his new leash. "Hi! Lovely to see you both."

Winter sunshine shone through bare branches as they walked away from the village. Anthony gestured to the small paw prints of a fox in the muddy track. "Hope he isn't heading for Ted's chickens!"

He wore his stockman hat, and waxed jacket over thick cord pants, tucked into his gumboots. Patricia was comfortable in her old blue rain jacket, soft jeans, and her muddy gumboots. She did not need a hat, but it was in one pocket, with her gloves in the other. Her short white hair gleamed, and she wore a touch of warm pink lipstick. Anthony passed a handful of small dog treats to put in her pocket for later. "I took Hannibal into the pet store to buy the longest leash they had. He met three other dogs and chose his own treats."

Patricia laughed. "Dog Heaven! I bet he couldn't believe his nose."

Anthony pressed the button to allow Hannibal to go further, but he immediately bounced on Sophie in play and knocked her off her feet. Again.

"Hannibal, no!" Anthony reeled his dog in and made him sit. "Sorry!"

Sophie shook herself and moved around to the other side of Patricia, who gave her a treat. "You will need to anticipate Hannibal being boisterous and defend yourself."

Anthony waited until Hannibal was still before he praised him and gave him a treat. They walked on, and across the fields in the distance, they could see the spire of St. Mary's church. "Mrs. Jessop says you both worship at St. Mary's in Chipping Hanley."

"We both sing in the choir."

"Does your choir need another bass, do you think?"

Patricia turned to him in delight, "What choir doesn't need another bass? It would be great to have you!"

After a great walk, avoiding the worst of the deep mud, they came back along a different path and neared the village again. Patricia found a fallen tree that was just the right height to sit on and drink tea. She offered clean water to Sophie and Hannibal from a portable dog dish. Sophie drank but Hannibal preferred a muddy puddle. He was behaving well, snuffling through the bushes on a long leash as Patricia took the flask out of her backpack and poured tea. Anthony fastened the line of the long leash in a diagonal across his body to free his hands and took the mug in his right hand. "You think of everything!"

He accepted a cookie in the other hand and was just about to sip the hot beverage when Patricia saw a rabbit emerge further along the path. Hannibal saw it too.

"Look out!"

Patricia jumped up as Hannibal bounded away. The leash snaked out, and she flung her arms around Anthony, shouting, "Brace! Brace!"

The huge dog reached the end of the line and was stopped in midair by their combined weight. All his paws came off the ground at the same time as the harness spun him around. There was an almighty jerk on the leash. Anthony's right arm flew upward and an arc of tea flew over their heads. The look of astonishment on his face as he stared into the empty mug set Patricia off laughing. Her arms were still around him and she started to let go when Hannibal bounded back toward them. The tension on the lease slackened and Anthony clutched at Patricia. He began to topple backward. They both struggled to stay upright, but his foot slipped, and he went down, pulling Patricia on top of him. Air expelled from both their lungs as they landed.

"Oof!"

The dogs bounced around them, Hannibal barking joyfully as if it was a new game.

It was chaos. They were both winded, and trying to angle her body off Anthony's, Patricia caused him to gasp again. Startled brown eyes looked up into hers. She studied his face as he studied hers. Her gaze skimmed down to his mouth and back up again. Anthony's eyes crinkled with laughter and he gasped, "Patricia, this is delightful, but we mustn't keep meeting like this. Can you lean up a bit and I will release Hannibal."

Hands braced on his broad chest, Patricia pushed backward, so Anthony could undo the clip of the leash and he breathed easier. "Could you manage to get off me without falling into the mud?"

Patricia nodded and looking over her shoulder, she walked her hands alternately down his thighs. Pink with embarrassment, she used his body as a bridge and struggled to her feet. Hannibal continued to bark as Patricia picked up both leashes and tied them to the tree. "Be quiet, Hannibal! Sophie, lie down."

Order returned to the clearing and Patricia turned, expecting to see Anthony on his feet, but he was stuck in a rut. He had been squashed deep by both their weights. His arms and legs thrashed as he tried to turn over and he looked so like a beetle that she chuckled. He looked at her from under the brim of his muddy hat. "Could you give me a hand up?"

Patricia hurried to plant her feet on his. She reached down as he reached up. "Ready? One, two, three!"

With a vigorous effort, Anthony came to his feet. They released hands, and he grinned awkwardly at her. "Sorry about that."

"Sorry?"

Patricia shook with laughter. She could no longer keep it in, howled and bent double, "Sorry! Oh my!"

Anthony started to laugh too, a hearty guffaw which started Hannibal barking again. Patricia wiped tears from her eyes as he peered over his shoulder at the back of his coat, which dripped mud and soggy leaves. He straightened his hat and squared his shoulders, which set Patricia off again. Her knees felt weak and she sat down on the log once more. It was probably the physical effort of pulling a man to his feet, but she felt excited and silly, like a fourteen-year-old girl. "Thank goodness no one from the village came along. This calls for more tea and cookies."

"More? I haven't had any tea yet, and Hannibal has eaten my cookie." He looked so mournful that Patricia laughed again as she gave him another mug of tea. He drank and munched, flexing his shoulders to lose some of the loose mud. "Mrs. Jessop should take a photo of this jacket and I will send it to the manufacturers. They designed it for the wet. I bet they have never seen someone wearing it as the airbag in a dog crash. Mrs. Jessop will wonder what on earth we have been up to."

By the time they walked back to their starting point, the sun had set in brilliant reds and oranges. In the chilly twilight Patricia grinned at the muddy dog and equally muddy man. "Goodnight."

"Goodnight. Thank you for tea and a most interesting walk. See you at church tomorrow."

Still laughing, Patricia hurried home with Sophie. People reacted to situations in such different ways. Ron would have been furious at the loss of his dignity, but Anthony was jolly. St. Mary's choir was fun already, but she looked forward to him being a member. Turning her thoughts to dinner, Patricia was grateful to live now. How did poor people in other centuries gone by cook and keep kids warm with just an open fire? She intended to light the log fire when she got home. It was an extra comfort, and she would cook dinner quickly on an electric stove.

* * *

Sophie pricked up her ears and Patricia heard the appalling noise before they reached the bend in Church Lane. It was dark. The white van and trailer were still parked in front of the cottages. Lights blazed from every window in Number 2 and rap music, her least favorite of any sound, blasted the night.

A big man stood in the front yard, next to a Harley-Davidson motorcycle. Despite the cold, he wore just a T-shirt over baggy jeans. Rolls of flesh flopped over the waistband and brawny arms were entirely covered in artwork tattoos. He watched with narrowed eyes as Patricia squeezed past the van with Sophie.

"Good evening, I'm Patricia from next—"

He ignored her and shouted, "DONNA!"

The upstairs window opened, and Donna shouted back, "WHAT?"

"Where do you want these boxes?"

"In the kitchen."

The window shut with a snap. The man picked up a box and carried it in through the open front door. Who was he? What was going on?

Confused and alarmed, Patricia took Sophie back to her cottage and trundled the yard cart to fetch more logs. Coming back up the path, she saw a Goth figure in the light from the kitchen. A youth dressed all in black sat on a patio chair, his eyes glued to the blue screen of his phone. A wing of black hair obscured half of his face, and when he moved, light reflected off multiple studs in his ears, nose, and bottom lip.

Patricia took the logs indoors, lit the fire, and toweled Sophie clean. She fed her, but the incessant bass notes beat through the wall, and she was getting a headache. Before making dinner, she would take the cookies next door and ask them to turn the music down. Patricia put the fireguard in place. "Stay, Sophie."

Only a double mattress still leaned against the outside wall. She negotiated packing trash and knocked on the front door. Tracey answered it, carrying the baby, and holding a lighted cigarette. Down the hallway, Patricia made eye contact with a tall, thin man. He had a huge, square beard and angry, black eyes. He cursed and walked out of her view. Bewildered, she held the plate out. "I made you some cookies and wondered, please could you turn the music down?"

Tracey said nothing. She turned and walked back to the kitchen as another woman came down the stairs. Patricia did a double take. It was Donna. But this did not look like the same Donna as her tenant. This one wore a short red skirt over leggings and high-heeled boots. A low-cut top accentuated every curve. Donna's hair, released from the tight bun, exploded in a cloud around her head and she wore heavy makeup. This made her look younger, but tough, and Patricia gulped. "I made cookies for you. I am confused because we agreed to no smoking in the cottage. You gave me the impression you wanted the cottage for just the two of you, and the baby. There are three men here and a big motorcycle."

"That belongs to Darren, my partner."

"But you said neither you nor your daughter had partners."

Donna shrugged, "They come and go. I have had enough nosy landlords in the past to know I can have anyone I want to stay here, without asking permission."

The heavy biker man walked from the kitchen and Patricia stood aside to let him pass. Her breath came fast, and she could not think. He grabbed the mattress, hoisted it over one shoulder and pushed his way past her into the cottage. She and Donna watched as he heaved it up the stairs, shoving and swearing, until he arrived on the landing.

Donna stepped closer to Patricia, speaking loudly above the pounding of the music. "That's Darren. The baby's father is in the kitchen with Tracey and the other one is my son. Not that it is any of your business. I know my rights. The Tenancy Agreement does not say who can live here, nor nothing about not smoking. I can peaceably hold and enjoy the Dwelling, without interruption by the Landlord."

She said this last sentence as if she knew it by heart from an official document. "Don't come around here again or I will file a police complaint for harassment. Thanks for the cookies."

She took the plate from Patricia's frozen hands and kicked the door shut in her face.

Chapter 9

Patricia spent the rest of the weekend going backwards and forwards between denial, anger, and depression. She was a fool. She had done this to herself. There was no one to call and ask for sympathy.

The incessant bass beat accompanied dinner until Patricia found some earplugs in the medicine cabinet. She put a noise-cancelling headset over the top. There were no earplugs for dogs and Sophie shook her ears, as if they hurt. What on earth was she to do?

Patricia started researching *tenants behaving badly* and learning all the things she should have known before allowing anyone to take over her cottage for a year! Later, she and Sophie did a walk around the churchyard before bed and it was a relief to remove the earplugs and get out of the cottage! The van and trailer were still there when Patricia set her phone alarm for the next morning. It was her turn to pick up Sarah for church. She slept lightly with Sophie on the floor next to her, but they both jumped wide awake at 2:27 a.m.

The engine of the van roared. Headlights outlined the beard of the angry man in the driver's seat. Patricia sat up in bed, pulled Sophie up onto the bed to hug and sit wrapped in her bedcovers, watching him. He tried to back the van along the lane but jack-knifed the trailer into the tree. He put it into forward gear and the van hit her fence. Patricia winced, but luckily, the fence withstood the blow. The man climbed out of the van, cursing. He unhitched the trailer and pushed it along the lane. A few minutes later, with screaming tires, he reversed the van up the lane. Patricia closed her window against the exhaust fumes. With his departure, the loud beat from next door stopped. She took out her earplugs but could not sleep. She lay wide awake with everything swirling around in her brain.

She must have dropped off to sleep at some point as the alarm woke her at 7:00 a.m. Frosty sunshine glittered outside and for a moment it was Groundhog Day, the fresh Saturday before the tenants arrived. Rubbing gritty eyes, Patricia let Sophie out into the backyard and stood under the shower with water pounding on her head. Next door was silent. After breakfast it felt safe to leave Sophie while she went to church, as she normally did on Sunday. But the morning was a blur.

She picked up Sarah, who was full of Anthony, Hannibal, and the mud. "What a state they were in when they got back! Anthony washed Hannibal in the downstairs shower and said they had the best time. How are things going with your tenants?"

"Noisy. But I expect they will settle down in a day or two. Anthony said he's joining St. Mary's choir."

The lanes were frosty, and Patricia needed to concentrate on her driving so was glad that Sarah talked and enthused about Anthony. Suddenly, they were in St. Mary's parking lot, but she did not remember driving there. Sarah jumped out. "Anthony's walking Hannibal, but he's following in a few minutes."

The white 4 x 4 arrived just before they started choir practice.

In the Service, Patricia prayed for guidance, but nodded off to sleep in Tim's sermon. Her head sank to her chest and she jerked up quickly. Across from Patricia, in the men's choir stalls, Anthony looked straight at her and smiled. It was the kindest, most understanding smile and she dropped her head again, to stop tears prickling in her eyes. Sarah invited her to lunch at the Manor House, but Patricia used Sophie as an excuse. She could not face more questions about the tenants. She had done stupid things in the past and would sort this one too.

Donna's car stood in front of the cottages. She and Tracey were putting the baby and stroller into the car. Patricia approached. "Hi Donna. I asked that you park at St. Peter's. Please leave your car there when you come back."

Tracey got into the passenger side. Donna climbed into the driver's seat and put the window down. "This is loading and unloading for the baby. You can't expect anyone to walk to that parking lot and back all the time." She started the engine and her voice was cold. "Your card said to be happy in our new home. I pay the rent; this is our home; and we are happy. Suck it up."

She swept the car in a tight circle and just made it past the tree. Patricia went over and gently touched the wound inflicted by the van. She could re-paint the long scrape along the fence, but she grieved for the tree and her lovely cottage. The biker man had taken the motorcycle but left patches of oil on the flattened grass. Packaging littered the yard, and Patricia saw now that Donna and her family intended to do their own thing. She thought she was a fair judge of character, but she had got it terribly wrong this time. She had wanted to help, but they had abused her trust. Sadder and wiser, she went indoors to be with Sophie.

Later that night, Darren and the motorcycle returned with a roar and Donna parked her car in front of the cottages. Sunday night was noisy, and she wore the earplugs and headset and worked on her plans for St. Peter's out-reach. She then took Sophie for a blissfully normal walk through the village. They had a delicious dinner of roast pork, vegetables, gravy, and applesauce.

Later, her computer offered fresh insights into why a safer option was leasing through an agent. Patricia laughed ruefully at herself. Being a *do-gooder,* she had naively signed the Tenancy Agreement with Donna. The people next door were of the dark. She was best in the early morning, and tomorrow was another day.

* * *

Monday morning was sunny and silent. Patricia dressed in her verger's robe and took Sophie with her to St. Peter's. Putting the tenants to the back of her mind, Patricia eagerly anticipated her long-awaited meeting with Tim Fell.

He was late.

St. Mary's, in Chipping Hanley, was Tim's biggest parish. Even before St. Peter's closed it was small in comparison and Patricia knew Tim was often waylaid. Sophie was nosing around in the robing room and disturbed a mouse. It skittered across the floor and she chased it to somewhere else. Patricia rolled up her sleeves and removed a nest from the Communion cupboard in the Robing Room. She pondered why mice did not bother her, but that she had a totally irrational fear of spiders?

Cleaned and smelling fresh, the cupboard contained only the vessels for bread and wine. When she went to wash her hands, she shuddered in the grim utility of the restroom. To cheer herself, she thought of new plumbing and bathroom fixtures, fresh paint, and color. It will be somewhere people WANT to go to wash their hands when I have finished with it! But she reminded herself, first we need to get people to come back. Sophie was sitting with her, but now dashed back into the church. Patricia guessed that Tim had arrived.

He leaned his bike inside the front door. "Sorry, I'm late. The roads are icy."

Tim wore no hat, and the tops of his ears glowed pink. Warm in the thermal layers beneath her robe, Patricia grinned as he unwound his big scarf. "No heating, remember?"

He grinned back at her and rewound the scarf. The Reverend Timothy Fell, Doctor of Theology, did not look like a minister. He was in his thirties, six feet tall and clean shaven. He had a broad face, with a strong nose and wide mouth, one corner of which often twitched when things amused him. Tim had short, blond hair and candid, blue-grey eyes that shone from behind rimless glasses. As usual, he wore jeans, Dr. Martens boots, and a tan leather jacket, much battered and comfortable. Under his scarf was a white ecclesiastical collar. Tim had confessed to Patricia once that he wanted to marry, when the right woman came along. "I love my life as a minister. It is a calling. I pray, but have yet to meet a young woman interested in dating a minister."

As they walked up the central aisle, Tim asked, "How are you? What have you been up to?"

Patricia did not want to answer the first question, so she pointed up at the window with *Jesus, Light of the World.*

"I have been cleaning for the past two weeks and really want to start on the outreach program. I've also got some questions about the church."

Tim sat down in a pew and gazed toward the altar. "You have done a lot and it looks great. Could you give me just a minute?"

He bent his head in prayer, and Patricia slipped into the pew behind him. She rested, her mind blank until Tim turned and placed his arm along the back of the pew. "This job is so busy that I sometimes lose sight of our Lord. Okay, I am with you. Start with a question and we'll go from there."

"Easy one. Is this original?"

Patricia led him to the right aisle, at the side of the altar, where a magnificent white sarcophagus filled the entire space. Side by side, the marble figures of Sir George Bartlett-Brown, and his wife, Anne, deceased 1581, lay under the carved canopy. Both faces were serene, their hands were folded upon their chests, and their feet rested upon a little dog. But along the wall behind them, was a ghastly cartoon in black stick figures. A line of skeletons danced from one end of the tomb to the other, led by the grinning figure of Death, who wore a crown.

Tim nodded. "It is original. In the sixteenth century they drew it into the plasterwork to remind us that, however rich and powerful, we are all mortal."

The iron latch on the door clicked, and Patricia turned in surprise. There had not been a single visitor since she started, and her face crinkled in delight as she hurried to greet Anthony. "How nice of you to come and see what we're doing!"

"Good morning." Anthony bent to pat Sophie. He was warmly dressed in a blue pea jacket with grey slacks. No hat, but gloves and a big grey scarf. He took off his glove to shake hands with Tim. Patricia stared. She gathered that he knew Anthony was joining them but had said nothing? Tim took off his glasses and polished them. "St. Peter's is lucky. We have an excellent verger and now, a new churchwarden as well."

What?

Tim turned to her. "Sorry, I need to rush away. I must get back for St. Mary's Parish Council meeting. Anthony knows more about the history of his family church than I do, so I will leave you in his capable hands. You could call me later to continue our conversation."

Speechless, Patricia nodded, and Tim opened the church door. He wheeled the bike out, calling goodbye as he walked down the path. Anthony was oblivious to her puzzlement. "We didn't have time to talk at church yesterday or we could have met up here in the afternoon. I am impressed, the church looks so much better than when I last saw it."

Patricia choked. "Were you here with Tim yesterday?"

Anthony set off down the side aisle. "No, I have my own set of keys. It is great, being the verger here, that you are interested in the family history. Shall we make a start?"

Patricia was treated to the Bartlett-Brown royal tour. Anthony was enthusiastic. "Of course, you know that the Duke built St. Peter's in the fourteenth century. Perhaps you did not know that the stained-glass windows to finish the church were imported at great cost by the Bartlett-Brown family."

He moved along to the wall of wooden boards; commemorating Bartlett-Browns killed in wars. "This one, John Bartlett-Brown, Captain, the King's Own Horse Regiment, was our great-great-grandfather. My brother, David, was the last to join that Regiment, now riding tanks, not on horses."

He was getting into his stride, but Patricia was desperate to call Tim. At an appropriate pause, she glanced at her watch. "This is fascinating, but I must go. Perhaps we could finish the story another time?"

"I would love that, and if you are in a hurry, I can lock up."

Anthony pulled out a ring of keys, identical to hers. "I am working on obedience with Hannibal today, but hoped we might go for a walk with you soon?"

Patricia had clipped on Sophie's leash and was heading for the door. "Lots of things are happening at the moment, and I... I am not sure of my week."

"That's okay," Anthony called after her, "I will be here

tomorrow, and the next day. We can compare calendars then."

* * *

Clear of the churchyard, Patricia called Tim on his mobile. He answered in three rings. "I am still cycling back. I knew you would call, so I have stopped in a gateway. I am so sorry I couldn't explain things before Anthony arrived."

"I don't understand. St. Peter's does not even have a congregation, but now there is a verger *and* a churchwarden?"

Tim's voice was gentle. "The Bishop called just before I left, and it was what I prayed about when I arrived. There was no time to discuss things, so I placed it in God's hands. I knew it would upset you, but Anthony is passionate about St. Peter's too and has given a large sum of money toward restoration."

"But I have started a fund-raising campaign with people in the village."

"I mentioned that to the Bishop. He reminded me it is the Bartlett-Brown ancestral church and Anthony paid for the roof repairs and CCTV."

Patricia's heart raced. She took a deep breath. "Then Anthony is churchwarden. But who is in the lead if you are not around?"

Tim sounded puzzled. "Ongoing, he also pays the verger's and groundsman's wages. This is not like you, Patricia. We are all part of the same team. He is seeking a new identity and I thought you would welcome him, on behalf of our Lord."

Patricia was contrite. "Yes, of course. We will work it out together."

Tim said goodbye. Patricia clicked off her phone and walked home with Sophie. After working all her life, with men as *the Boss*, she now worked for Anthony Bartlett-Brown, financier, and businessman. Patricia found that she did not care about his identity, since hers had just been demolished.

Chapter 10

On Tuesday morning, Patricia took Ted to the Medical Center. He was of the generation that wore their best clothes to see the doctor. In Ted's case it was dark pants with a crease down the front, blue shirt, collar, and tie. On top, he wore his best winter coat, with polished, lace-up shoes, and Clair tied a paisley-patterned scarf around his neck. She tried to put his hat on the neatly combed white hair, but he batted her hand away, "Clair, stop it! I am not a baby."

Patricia settled him into the passenger seat of the Morris and leaned across to plug in his seat belt. They waved to Clair as they drove up the lane. Ted took his hat off with one hand and pulled the seatbelt away from his chest. "I don't hold with wearing hats in cars; and why do they make these things so tight?"

He gazed out at the winter fields as they drove toward Banbury. "It's nice to see everything again."

He chuckled. "I hear you're helping to train the idiot with the sniffer dog. How's that going?"

"Ted," Patricia turned her head for a moment to grin at him, "be kind! Although…"

She had not intended telling anyone about St. Peter's with Tim and Anthony. But it weighed heavily on her mind.

She suddenly told Ted everything. "There's not enough work for two of us. It's like some bizarre marriage."

"Shame you never had a marriage like me and May."

Emptied of outrage, Patricia laughed. "Ted, no one had a marriage like you and May!"

"That's true but I warned you about Anthony. I like David, but that Anthony was always a Mummy's boy."

Patricia maneuvered the car through the traffic. "I thought he lost his mother when he was young?"

Ted nodded, "Florence, her name was, nice lady, I remember her. Anthony was about ten when she died. George, his father, shunted him off to boarding school. Anthony followed him into the business, but never got much approval, so David told me. George married again and Anthony became a workaholic in London. He's stinking rich, but has never been interested in Summerfield."

Patricia was upset, but always tried to be fair. "Tim said Anthony paid for the repairs to St. Peter's and had CCTV installed. His tithing to the Oxford Diocese pays Jim's and my wages."

Ted considered this. "That's for the glory of the Bartlett-Browns, not the village. Then he adopts a monster, damaged dog, a totally idiot choice for a place like Summerfield."

Patricia thought Hannibal was as much a damaged veteran as David and deserved a second chance. Ted was still brooding about his hens, so she changed the subject. "I have made a complete fool of myself with the tenants I gave my cottage to next door. I believed the woman was down on her luck, and I have had a lot of help over the years. I wanted to give something back and it was all positive until I handed over the keys. Then I find she is an accomplished actress. She is aggressive, and the constant, loud noise is blowing my mind."

Eyes on the road ahead, Patricia did not notice that Ted had dozed off. She stopped speaking and after a few minutes he sat up and his eyes opened. "You can tell me anything. I know how efficient you are, and you will find a way around it. Besides, you've got something more serious to worry about."

Patricia signaled to turn right into the Medical Center. Alarmed, she glanced at him while they waited for the traffic lights to change. "What now?"

"Jim fancies dating you."

She did not know whether to laugh or cry. "Excuse me? I only know him as the groundsman for St. Peter's."

"I am telling you this in confidence. Jim's my friend and we both lost our wives to cancer. But he is ready to marry again and is interested in 'that nice lady verger,' who lives at Number 1, Halfmoon Cottages."

He chuckled when Patricia gasped. She drove into the Medical Center and parked in the Disabled Parking Space. "Oh, dear me, and I bought him a takeaway coffee from the Market."

Patricia fetched a wheelchair and settled Ted into it. He squeezed her hand. "I've heard you say before that you don't want to marry again, but Jim hasn't heard that. He's serious. Go on a date if you want to, but Jim thinks all women play hard to get. He won't give up if you give him any hope."

A nurse trundled Ted off for tests and Patricia sat down in the Waiting Room. Jim did not raise even a tiny sparkle of anything. Anthony, even though she was furious with him, was at least an attractive man. Patricia picked up a women's magazine, but the articles for older women annoyed her. *How to look your best for an older romance.*

The last thing she wanted was an older romance! Patricia turned to the food pages, but one picture had caught her attention. She turned back to look at it again. A happy older couple walked along a beach, hand in hand. The woman had white hair and blue eyes, like her. Patricia read the caption.

It is never too late to find someone special to share walks and beautiful places. Best of all, to be with someone you love, and who loves you.

Ted came back from X-ray and they went into the consulting room. The doctor was in his late twenties, with a mop of brown hair and designer glasses. He did not wear a white coat, but beige chinos and a sweater with his name badge. He shook hands with them, and Patricia took a chair against the wall, to leave Ted in charge. "Good afternoon, doctor. My granddaughter is at work, so our friend, Mrs. Anderson, has brought me."

The doctor perched on a corner of his desk, holding a sheaf of lab reports. "Excellent news, Mr. Williams. We can offer you a triple bypass heart operation in Oxford next week, on the National Health Service. You will be in and out of the hospital before Christmas."

Having given this amazing gift, he waited expectantly. Ted stared down at his polished shoes on the footrests of the wheelchair, then raised his head. "Thank you, doctor. I appreciate the offer, but I do not want surgery. It is too late, and I will not go voluntarily into that or any other hospital. My wife, May, died in the Oxford hospital. At Summerfield Stables, we treat animals with more kindness."

The doctor was taken aback. He went around to his chair and sat down. "Could you tell me some more about that?"

Ted's eyes filled with tears. "The vet shot Russ, my best horse, with a humane killer. It was dark, he was in his own stall, and not afraid. My granddaughter and me, we loved him. We put our arms around him. Then he went home, to the green fields of his own heaven."

Patricia breathed deeply to hold back a sob as Ted went on, "My wonderful wife, May, who had such courage, was afraid in that hospital. She had tubes coming out of everywhere. They would not let me stay the night with her, so she died alone."

The young doctor took off his glasses and rubbed his eyes. "I'm so sorry, Mr. Williams. What can I do to help you?"

Ted shifted uncomfortably in the wheelchair. He was thin now and bruised easily. "I know hospitals do wonderful work. My granddaughter's husband had a leg amputated and walks well with his prosthetic. One day soon, my old heart will stop, and that is how it should be. It has been a miracle to live so well, for so long. I am tired all the time. I should like to manage without pain, so as not to distress my granddaughter. I want to die at home. Can you help me do that?"

The doctor picked up his prescription pad. He came around the desk and pulled up a chair next to Ted. "I can prescribe painkillers and arrange for a district nurse to come regularly. We have trained caregivers who can attend morning and evening, to help with your washing and medication."

They discussed details and Patricia excused herself to go to the restroom. She put her hands on the sink and looked at her face in the mirror. She ached, thinking back to Ron at the end of his life, and her parents before that. She would not have wished it any other way but saw the path ahead for Clair.

Patricia splashed water on her face and refreshed her lipstick. She would help in whatever way she could. When she found Ted, he was at the Pharmacy, being briefed on his medications.

* * *

Driving home, Patricia was moved to say, "The doctor was surprised. People do not turn down surgery that will prolong their life. Especially if they do not need thousands of pounds to pay for it."

Ted smiled with tired eyes. "I am not *people,* am I? Death is natural, like birth. I do not want one of those defibrillator things thumping me off the bed. I want peace at night and my dog to comfort me."

He was quiet for the rest of the journey, hands folded in his lap. As they entered Summerfield, he said, "I need you to promise not to tell Clair about the surgery. She lost her mum, dad, her little brother, and then her grandma. She is afraid of losing me. If she knew about the bypass, she would cry. Then I would have the operation, just to make her happy, but I don't want it. Promise?"

"I promise."

Patricia parked, and Ted sighed with relief. Leaning on his cane and holding Patricia's arm, he walked slowly through the arched gate in the wall to his familiar garden. Ted Williams looked at the pretty cottage where he was born and smiled. He was home.

* * *

Patricia texted Clair when she got back to the car.

Hi! Ted in bed with warm beverage and all good.
New doctor and new meds. District Nurse will contact you about home caregivers.
Hope you're okay, have left Sophie with Joss and Ted--will collect on my way home. In urgent need of afternoon tea and CAKE in Oxford!

Patricia felt the weight lift as she drove. The tenants were a problem and Anthony, a nuisance, but she was in good health and free! She wanted to wander aimlessly through graceful old buildings and be among crowds of people getting ready for Christmas.

Parking was always difficult in Oxford and she circled tiny back streets until she found a space. It was a grey day, chilly and cloudy, but not raining. She walked through the colleges on her way to the shops and breathed. Lights shone from high Gothic windows onto neat gravel paths and mown grass lawns. At the entrance to Christ Church college, porters were erecting Christmas trees and hanging twinkling lights.

Patricia strolled through brightly lit stores. There were still seven weeks until the holiday, but store owners had already stuffed windows with goodies. They seemed to start earlier every year! Halloween was gone in a pile of carved pumpkins. People were collecting fallen branches from Potlatch Wood for the communal bonfire in Summerfield tomorrow night. They would light it and let off fireworks. Firecrackers terrified Sophie so she would close the drapes and turn the TV volume up. For now, it was time for tea, tiny sandwiches, and Victoria sponge cake in her favorite teashop.

* * *

When she had collected Sophie, they walked down to Half-moon Cottages in darkness and blessed silence. Donna's car and the motorcycle were both gone. Patricia let herself into Number 1, locked the doors, and closed the drapes in the sitting room. Sidelamps on, the room glowing, soon flames crackled through dry cherry logs in the fireplace. After feeding Sophie, Patricia sat on the couch with her laptop. "I shall write a list of what I can do about the tenants, Sophie. If they will not compromise, I shall have to evict them. It will be another expense, but it is my fault. Next time I will work with an agency."

She leaned back on the couch cushions and thought about her family. Finishing her tea in Oxford, Patricia called and managed to get through to Charlotte. They spoke briefly and Patricia asked if Daddy was there. She wished she could ask Paul's advice about the tenants, but he was in China again. With Christmas coming, was there any way she could mend the breach?

Patricia bent to stroke Sophie and opened her emails. There was a reply from the Citizen's Advice Bureau. "Oh, good."

She opened the attachment which stated that she could not apply for an Eviction Order unless the tenant had specifically broken the Tenancy Agreement in the following ways:

- Non-payment of rent

- Property used for illegal activity

- Damage/nuisance to neighbors

- Verbal/physical threats to Landlord

Patricia pushed the laptop to one side and massaged her forehead with both hands. It looked like months of misery ahead if those things were likely to happen. Surely things must improve. But, if not, could she live in such a situation? Maybe she and Sophie should just move out? But where could they go? The answer in her head came back, loud and clear.

You do not have enough money to move. There is nowhere else to go.

Chapter 11

Patricia was in bed and asleep at 2:00 a.m. when the tenants came home. The motorcycle engine roared, Donna's car doors slammed, and the baby howled. Harsh voices shouted. Within minutes of going inside, loud, heavy beat music vibrated through the walls.

Silence at 5:00 a.m., but Patricia had not slept again. She got up, put on her comforting verger's outfit, and went out in the dark with Sophie to seek sanctuary at St. Peter's. They turned the corner and all the lights were on inside the church.

Anthony wielded a pickaxe. He was ripping out rotten floorboards by the organ. More noise!

He saw them and stopped, face alight with pleasure. "Good morning! I was awake, so I thought I would start work."

He bent to caress Sophie's head. "Hannibal is in his crate in the 4 x 4. He's not as well-behaved as Sophie and I cannot work with him here. I thought I would do an hour before it's light, then take him for a walk."

Anthony had on tough, lace-up boots, heavyweight navy dungarees, and a thick sweater. He indicated the space, cleared from the organ to the back room showing all the rot. "What do you think? I had the pews moved into that back room yesterday. A master carver carved them, but they need cleaning. We can put them back after they replace the floor."

Patricia felt a flush of resentment. She had planned for the removal of the pews and replacement of the floor. But Anthony leaned on his pickaxe and looked pleased with himself. "I've recruited David and Jim for the bell ringing team. The Lead ringer from St. Mary's is coming over to check the bells and give us a lesson."

The look on her face stopped Anthony enthusing. "I thought you'd be pleased…"

Patricia had resolved to work harmoniously with him, but she was tired and crabby. "What should I be pleased about? The only thing you have left for me is more cleaning. You did not talk to me first, you just did it."

She was about to walk away in disgust when she spotted a rusty, iron plate. It was perforated with small holes and half hidden by the foot of the organ. "What is that?"

Anthony bent to look. "Goodness me, that is the air vent into the Bartlett-Brown crypt. I've never seen it from this side before."

He seemed puzzled he had upset her and tentatively asked, "I know you like church history, have you seen the crypt yet?"

Patricia knew all her keys to all the doors. There was not one for a crypt, so she shook her head.

"Cathedrals like St. Paul's in London and York Minster have crypts for royalty, but there are few crypts under small churches. I could show you now if you want."

Patricia shelved her resentment because she wanted to see the crypt. She smiled. "Thanks, I should like that."

"My personal key is back at the Manor House, but there's another in the safe."

Safe? What safe?

If Tim knew about it, he had not shared this information with her, either. Had she stumbled into a secret boys' club?

Patricia followed Anthony into the robing room. The ceremonial vestments for the minister hung in an old corner closet, and he reached inside. There was a click and Patricia leaned in, to see an open panel at the back. Anthony keyed in numbers, a safe opened, and he handed her a key fob like her own, embossed with the crossed keys of St. Peter's. She fought back indignation. *This was the verger's symbol and those keys should be on her ring.*

There were two keys, one was iron, big and old; the other was a modern, deadlock key. She closed her hand around them. Anthony reached into the safe again and reverently lifted something out, wrapped in a soft linen cloth. He whispered, "Patricia, hold out your hands."

It was said in such a tender tone that she immediately obeyed. Anthony transferred the object and cradled her hands in his. "It is heavy, and we must not let it drop. It is priceless; so rare that it cannot be insured."

He slid the covering away. In her hands, Patricia held a gold cross, about twelve inches long, on a small square base. It was exquisite. The gold was pure and perfectly crafted. The jeweler had mounted sapphires and pearls all around the base. Patricia let out her breath in a soft sigh, "I have seen nothing so beautiful, not even in a church museum, and your family own it?"

Anthony was close, his hands supporting hers. He was an older man with a white beard, but his eyes had the wonder of a small boy. "It belonged to my mother, and she told me that monks made it in the fifteenth century. It is to remind us of the sacrifice, more precious than earthly gold, that was made upon a cross. Our family do not own it, we are custodians."

He looked into her eyes, "The sapphires are the same blue as my mother's eyes, the same blue as yours. I noticed when we first met at the Stables and hoped I might have the opportunity to show you this one day."

"Thank you." Patricia wondered how he managed to cause such emotional turmoil in her heart. One minute she was furious with him. The next, she wanted to reach up and kiss him for his sweetness.

Anthony carefully wrapped the cross and replaced it in the safe. The panel clicked shut." Let me show you how to open it."

He reached for her hand and guided it. "Press the third carved rosette. The code is my mother's birthdate, on the plinth of her angel in the churchyard."

Anthony led out of the church. Dawn had broken. It was cold and raining again, but Patricia felt warmed by his trust. Around the back of the building, near the path leading to her cottage, Anthony lifted a curtain of ivy over some steep steps. Sophie and Patricia came to stand beside him. "I noticed these, but thought they led to the boiler room."

"I asked Jim not to trim this, to avoid attracting attention."

He turned the handle of a standard electricity box and flicked the Mains switch to ON. There was a faint ticking from the meter. "One time I came down here and forgot to switch this off. The lights were on for a year before my next visit, so I had a thirty-minute timer put in. I am glad we are looking today, in case there are any repairs needed. If not, we can lock it up for another year."

He started down the steps, holding onto the iron handrail and Patricia followed. But Sophie pulled back at the end of the extending leash and Patricia went back up again. "It's okay, girl, no worries."

She wrapped the leash around the handrail and wedged the handle of her umbrella, so the spokes rested on the ground on one side. Sophie sat in a little tent. "Stay there and I will be back in a few minutes."

Anthony unlocked the faded grey door at the bottom of the steps and went in. Patricia followed, apprehensive but excited. She had visited Windsor Castle, where they buried King Henry the Eighth in 1547, but had no idea St. Peter's had a historic crypt.

An overhead, neon strip light showed a dry concrete floor and a stainless-steel inner door. Anthony unlocked it with the modern key, and it slid smoothly to one side on hydraulic runners. "This is a bank security door, installed when I took my father's Power of Attorney. In 1693, the Bartlett-Browns lined the original stone vault with lead, as befitting the wealth of the family. Lead is worth a fortune now. It is good thieves do not hear about it; but they would find it impossible to get in if they tried."

Patricia drew in a breath and the air was musty but not damp. It embarrassed her to ask, "Are there spiders?"

Anthony stepped into the vault and looked around. "A few old cobwebs, but I cannot see any spiders."

Patricia stepped cautiously through the steel door, and his face crinkled into a smile. "I felt like that when I first came in. But it is just a mausoleum. They are historic tombs, but everything inside is dust."

The ceiling was higher than she expected. Anthony led her to the top end of the crypt. "Nearest to the altar was considered most holy. This is like the tomb upstairs but does not have the canopy or the dog."

Patricia added. "Or the skeleton cartoon."

Anthony pointed out the features of the table tombs, great stone boxes that stood in two parallel lines. Each had a carved marble figure or two on the top, hands pressed together in prayer. Patricia noticed another dog, a marble sculpture at the feet of a couple near the door.

Anthony pointed to a wide shelf on the opposite side of the crypt. "Those are relatively modern cremation jars, and look, there's the vent into the church."

A draft from the open door waved the curtain of cobwebs. Maybe it was lack of sleep, but Patricia clutched her stomach with cramping nausea. She looked for the quickest route to the door, desperate to get out before she threw up. She put her hand over her mouth and ran.

At the top of the steps, she fought the nausea and put the umbrella up over her and Sophie. Anthony locked up and came up the steps, then sat down on the top, Sophie between them. "Without meaning to, I have somehow upset you again."

Patricia shook her head and covered them all with the umbrella. "We had a sleepless night and being down there reminded me of *Romeo and Juliet,* buried in their tomb."

Anthony nodded. "I understand. My father had Mother buried in the crypt. I told him she hated being shut in. I begged him not to, but he is a stickler for Bartlett-Brown tradition and said I was a sentimental fool."

"There is no name on the angel sculpture in the churchyard."

"Archangel Michael was my mother's Guardian Angel. I commissioned the sculpture of him when Father retired and went permanently to live on his yacht. I had Mother's remains cremated, as she requested in her Will, and the ashes are mixed into the cement of the plinth. Her tomb is still down there but it is empty. Except for me and the funeral director, you are the only person who knows where she is."

Their hands were close together, both stroking Sophie, who was loving the attention. Patricia rested her hand on his. "You were too young to bear such grief."

Rain pattered on the enormous umbrella and gurgled down the drainpipe behind them. It was strangely intimate in the gloom beneath the umbrella. Anthony held her hand. "Mother and I shared so many things. I was away at school and considered too young to attend the funeral. Now I am retired, I want to renovate St. Peter's in her memory."

Patricia let go of his hand to pull a sheet of paper from her pocket. "Do you think your mother would have welcomed the people of Summerfield back to St. Peter's? My vision is to build a community, like St. Mary's, and Tim is supportive. Our aim is to welcome older folks and little ones, raise money for a minibus, so that groups could meet here. I drafted this notice to put on the board in the porch."

Anthony took the paper. Patricia kept the umbrella angled over them and listened as he read aloud.

Welcome to St. Peter's, Summerfield.

This beautiful church has stood for 700 years, to the glory of God, witnessing the faith of Christian men and women.

We seek to worship in an inclusive congregation, open to old and young, rich and poor, Summerfield-born, and new arrivals.

Our aim is, through Faith, to make a positive contribution in the parish.

Anthony put the paper down and his eyes were puzzled. "I thought I made it clear that this is our family church, my mother's church. My vision is to return it to how it was when she was alive, to make it a shrine for private prayer and contemplation."

He paused, "Besides, I doubt there are enough people who care about your vision, to make it happen."

Patricia jumped to her feet and Sophie leaped away, tail between her legs. "That is so not true!"

Anthony stood too and she glared at him. "There is only one bus a week to Banbury, and only one to Oxford. Many older folks are isolated on farms, mothers have nowhere to meet or let preschoolers play together. There are people who are out of work in Summerfield and young couples with children, living on Government food stamps. St. Peter's could offer them a hot meal, companionship, and a place to pray. We could be an outreach community, helping ordinary people to come together and maybe find their Faith."

"No."

Anthony strode away and the piece of paper fluttered to the ground. Patricia swooped to grab it as she and Sophie jogged after him. "That back room would be great as a Food Bank and visiting library. We could have a Mothers and Toddlers group on that bit by the organ, serve coffee, swap children's clothes and …"

Anthony turned and she saw the steel of a CEO, the Chief Executive Officer of his own company, the *Boss*. "I said, no."

Patricia's face was pink as she faced him. "I have already started involving people. With some material help and a quiet sanctuary, there is room here for spiritual growth. I have experienced it myself."

His face was stubborn and set. Fire flashed from her brilliant blue eyes. "You were so nice as Santa at the Stables; I see now it was an act. Underneath you are arrogant, and entitled, muscling in to play the 'Lord of the Manor.' You want to keep St. Peter's as an exclusive Bartlett-Brown shrine, gloating over your gold cross and the distinguished members of your family. Are you any different from your father? Is this what Lady Florence would have expected from her son?"

Patricia stood still and watched Anthony turn to walk away. "Tim made it clear, you pay the money, so you will make the decisions. But let me make it clear to you, I will not walk with you again. I shall email Tim and resign. It is all yours, Sir Anthony. There's not enough room at St. Peter's for us both."

Chapter 12

Patricia walked rapidly in the opposite direction from Anthony and sat on the bench by Ted's family grave. The rain had stopped but she felt safer with Sophie beneath the wing of her verger's umbrella. "Thank goodness I have you, Sophie, because nothing else is working in my life. Paul and his family do not want me, tenants from Hell have the cottage, and Anthony has taken St. Peter's."

The despair in her heart triggered tears. Sophie stood up and wagged her tail. Peeping out, Patricia saw Jim standing nearby, dripping in the rain. "Hi."

She brushed a hand across wet cheeks, as if wiping away raindrops. "'Morning, Jim. I won't say good morning because it is such dreadful weather again."

"But it is warmer when it's raining."

He wore his usual brown coverall, but today, there was a plastic sack over his shoulders.

"Does that keep out the wet?"

"Not much, but it's better than nothing. I put my old raincoat down somewhere. Are you okay? You looked sad when I came along the path."

"You know how it is… sometimes things get to you."

Patricia furled her umbrella and moved along the bench,

to make room for him to join her and Sophie. "How is Ted doing?"

Jim sat down. "He is frailer every time I see him. We watch sports on TV and then I go again."

"I am sure he appreciates you being there. I wanted to ask, are there many burials these days? I have arranged a wedding but not a funeral."

Jim pointed to the grave in front of them. "The last burial was May, Ted's wife. Her parents bought this plot when they got married. Folks did that back then. When Ted goes, he will join May and her parents. The ashes of Clair's family are in here too. But this graveyard is full now, so there will be no more burials."

Both Jim and Sophie smelled like wet dogs. Patricia stood up, ready to go home. Jim pulled thick gloves from his back pocket. "I came to do some clearing for you, where the Christmas roses are. I will do it as a volunteer, not as my paid work."

After the drama with Anthony, Patricia smiled, grateful for someone willing to help her. "How kind! Would you show me where they are?"

Brambles covered the oldest gravestones. Jim bent to pull a gigantic stinging nettle out of her way and suddenly, grabbed her arm. "Watch out for that hole!"

He released her, and Patricia peered into the dark opening by her feet. "Thank you. How long have you been a gravedigger here?"

Jim thought for a moment. "I can't remember exactly, but I worked with my dad when I was a teenager and took over when he died."

He pointed toward the crematorium Memorial Garden. "He and Mum are over there, and my wife. I lost her at the same time Ted lost May."

Patricia shook her head sadly. "I'm sorry for your loss. My husband died five years ago. We don't forget."

Jim guided her around a headstone leaning at a dangerous angle. "The yew trees cause settling and the ground sinks just here."

Sheltered by the wall, a flat gravestone had legible words and Patricia bent over to read them.

Elizabeth Anne Henderson
Died November 10, 1848
Aged 3 years and 10 weeks
Parents dear, do not lament
For I am gone to rest
God took me in my early years
To be forever blessed

Patricia thought of Paul, "How tragic! Are there more children's graves in this undergrowth?"

Jim nodded, "Victorian. They were wealthy but buried children they lost to diphtheria, smallpox, tuberculosis, and influenza. Sometimes two or three at the same time."

"We are lucky to live now, with greater knowledge and antibiotics."

"Doesn't stop death, though, does it? Look, there is the biggest patch of Christmas roses, and they are in bud!"

Patricia exclaimed but stepped back onto the path, out of the dangers beneath her feet. "I shall look forward to seeing them in bloom. Thanks so much for clearing them."

Sophie began to pull at her leash, her nose pointing back toward the church. "What's up, Soph?"

Was that a dog barking in the distance?

Jim cleared his throat. "Um… I wondered whether you would like to go to the Oxford Christmas Market with me? It's nice to walk around, and we could have a bite to eat afterwards."

Oh no!

Patricia froze. Self-consciously she twisted Ron's wedding ring. She had forgotten Ted's warning and allowed Jim the opportunity to ask her for a date! She could not think of the right words to refuse him, so he spoke again. "I know you are an independent lady. But you must get lonely sometimes, like I do. Will you come with me?"

Patricia would have said yes, just once, so as not to hurt his feelings, but she remembered Ted's words and steeled herself. "Thank you for asking and I am sorry to say no. I don't want to date anyone, so I hope you will excuse me."

Sophie leaped madly on the end of her leash, trying to go back to the church. Then Patricia recognized the distant barking. "I'm sorry to hurry away, but I think Hannibal is in trouble."

Sophie bounded forward and this time Patricia did not hold her back.

* * *

In Potlatch Wood, an unruly wind roared in the treetops. It had torn off a great branch which lay smashed on the path. Patricia climbed over it, holding the stitch in her side. Sophie pulled. She panted and jogged after her. The frantic barking was louder.

The wood ran alongside the field with St. Mary's spire in the distance. A five-bar gate topped a slope at the end of the track. In the deep gluey mud against the gate a gang of colossal Hereford steers surrounded Anthony and Hannibal, bellowing, and threatening them with lowered horns.

Anthony held the leash tight and was trying to pull Hannibal back. But the big dog was barking and plunging in the mud. The steers edged closer to them and Patricia ran. "Sophie, down. Stay!"

She sprang up the gate and leaned over the top bar. Steadying herself with her left hand on Anthony's shoulder, she whacked the lead steer hard on the nose with her umbrella. It threw up its head, bellowed, and backed two steps. With all her strength, Patricia shouted and hit all the noses she could reach. The cattle showed the whites of their eyes, churned the mud with their hooves, and moved back out of her reach. Patricia looked down to release the latch on the gate, but someone had padlocked it. "Anthony, quick, give me the leash!"

Anthony held up the blue handle. She grabbed it and released the extension button. Clambering off the gate she slid the leash along the top bar. "Hannibal, come!"

Covered in brown sludge, the black dog seemed only too glad to plunge toward her. The steers turned their heads and began to follow. Patricia's thought was to get him through the hedge. But the farmer had twisted three vicious strands of barbed wire from the gatepost to the next post and on, all around the field. Hannibal was too big to go over or between the strands. There was only one way. Patricia remembered a video on police dog training and prayed that Hannibal's army training had been the same. She pointed to the ground and commanded, "Down."

Hannibal dropped in the mud; his eyes fixed on her. Her hand in the signal for *Down*, Patricia knelt and held the strands of hawthorn hedge away from the wire. She leaned down to look at Hannibal underneath the bottom strand of wire. There was just enough room for him to get through if he stayed down. But would he? The steers were bellowing again and coming closer. A dog was a danger to them and they intended goring him with those murderous horns. Hannibal turned his head to look.

"No!"

Patricia remembered the bag of treats in her pocket and pulled them out, rustling the wrapper. "Hannibal, look!"

Hannibal saw them. Keeping her hand in the 'down' position, she commanded, "Come."

Glory be!

His belly flat to the mud, he crawled toward her and Patricia encouraged him. "Good boy! Stay down, now come!"

Hannibal crawled slowly under the razor-sharp barbs. He was so close that they snagged some hair, but not his flesh. Patricia grabbed his harness, hauled him the last foot, and into her arms. "Good dog! Oh, you good dog! You are such a clever boy!"

She hugged him hard and fed him treats. Cattle jostled on the other side of the wire, and *mooed* dolefully, with wide eyes and dripping noses. Patricia smoothed mud from Hannibal's face. She walked him back to Sophie, tied the leashes to a tree so Hannibal could not eat Sophie's treats and made a pile for each of them. Leaving them to chew, she hurried back to Anthony.

He had climbed the gate and stood with one boot on, the other still firmly stuck in the thick mud. He was white and shaking. "There have never been cattle in this field before. We did not see them until they galloped over the hill. One minute, there was an empty field, the next, they were backing us up against the gate. It was padlocked. It has never been padlocked. I could get over, but not with Hannibal."

Patricia sat down next to him. She was breathless and feeling drained as her adrenaline level dropped. She leaned back against the gate. "I am only glad you are okay. Cattle have killed people in that situation. Why didn't you let Hannibal off the leash? They would have chased him."

Anthony's face was haggard. "A farmer stopped me in the market and told me, if my dog went anywhere near his stock, he would have him shot. This could be his field."

But then a mud-splattered, smile lit his face and he reached for her hand. "But for you, we would have been trampled."

"Luckily, we had not gone home, and Sophie heard Hannibal. It was miraculous! Without that crawling thing, he would have been toast."

Patricia used the five bars of the gate to pull herself to her feet, "Come on. We need to get warm and dry as soon as possible or we will catch chills."

Two bullocks stared as she tentatively held out a hand to Anthony. The rest of the steers had wandered off. Wearily, Anthony took her hand and struggled to his feet. Patricia untied the dogs and they walked slowly back toward the cars.

Suddenly, Hannibal stopped and shook himself vigorously. Blobs of filth splattered all over Anthony. He looked down at himself and at Patricia, with a suggestion of the old twinkle in his eye. "Good one, Hannibal! All I need is to arrive home, covered in mud and wearing only one boot, to have Sarah look at me like last time!"

Limping along on one booted foot and a muddy sock, he took Patricia's arm and murmured, "Before the bullocks arrived, I was thinking about what you said. I have got set in my ways and fixated on my own agenda. You are right, Mother would have expected more of me. If she were alive, she would be there to offer a helping hand."

They reached the 4 x 4, and Anthony loaded Hannibal into his crate. He turned to face Patricia, "Please don't resign. St. Peter's needs you."

He paused and she saw the sincerity in his brown eyes. "I need you and Hannibal needs you. Could we meet tomorrow, to talk more about your vision?"

Chapter 13

Patricia swung the umbrella and danced a few steps with Sophie along Church Lane. She was shattered with fatigue, but there was hope. "Thank you, thank you, thank you!"

She did not want to resign but blurted it out in a moment of anguish. However, had Anthony not changed, she would have gone through with it because there would have been no future for her project. Patricia ached from poor sleep, climbing gates, and kneeling in the mud, but she glowed with possibilities. "Let's go in the back way, Sophie, and avoid being irritated by Donna's car. I'll get two more logs for tonight. This coat can soak in the washing machine, and I will soak in the bathtub!"

The tenants were silent until afternoon. Patricia mentally planned a delicious brunch with Sophie, and when they started the racket next door, she would put in earplugs and go back to bed. Later, she would take Sophie for a walk and review her ideas for St. Peter's to talk about with Anthony. Patricia turned from Church Lane onto the track behind Halfmoon Cottages and saw the sports shoes hanging by their laces over the power lines. She chuckled, remembering her schooldays, when boys did this with each other's sports shoes. "Someone will be in trouble when they get home."

She did not chuckle when she reached the woodstore. Heavy metal music already pounded from the cottage and she kicked a log in frustration. In through the back door, and the muddy coat went into the washing machine. Patricia changed into a grey fleece jogging suit and put in earplugs, but even the leaves of her indoor plants were vibrating. She screwed up her face. "There is nothing else to do, I must challenge them. I hate conflict, but if I am not strong, they will think this is okay."

Leaving Sophie in the kitchen, Patricia went out of her yard and in at the gate of Number 2. Darren sat with his legs under the motorcycle, tinkering with the engine. Mobile phone in hand, Goth Boy leaned on the windowsill and watched. He glanced at Patricia and disappeared behind the black hair. The music pounded out of the open front door.

"Excuse me…Darren, I need you to…"

He looked up with such contempt that he took her breath away. But she was determined to say what she had come to say. "Please, could you turn the music down? The bass vibrates through the wall and…"

Darren turned his head to Goth Boy. "Get your mother."

He turned back to the engine. The boy paused and momentarily made eye contact with Patricia before slipping away.

Was that sympathy she read in his eyes?

Donna came through the front door like a bat out of Hell. "Are you stupid or something? How many times do you need telling? Get out!"

Patricia maintained eye contact. "Your music is so loud that I need to wear earplugs. My dog's hearing is being damaged. I am asking you to turn the volume down, or I will report you to the police."

Donna advanced, her face livid, and Patricia flinched.

"Leave it, Donna."

Darren got up. He was a flabby hulk, but Donna stopped.

He turned to Patricia. "Some landlords don't understand at first, but you need to learn fast. This is our place and we do whatever we like in our place. Think hard before you call the police, or an accident could happen to that nice dog of yours."

Patricia went home and locked the doors. She closed the drapes against the ugliness next door. Earplugs in, she took a mug of tea upstairs with Sophie and ran a bath with lavender essence. In the tub, tears fell into the steamy water. Darren spoke softly, but his message was clear. Do as you are told, or he would hurt Sophie.

* * *

In bed, Patricia fell asleep. She woke several hours later and took out the earplugs. All was quiet. The car and motorcycle were gone.

She walked Sophie around St. Peter's. She would always need to be on her guard now and keep Sophie with her. Needing to hear a friendly voice, Patricia called Clair, but got her voicemail. She called Sarah next, who was home and congratulated her on the rescue. "Anthony was so admiring of how you handled that umbrella! You probably saved their lives."

"I must be mad! I ran, climbed the gate, and whacked cattle, as if I were twenty, not sixty-something. Are Anthony and Hannibal okay?"

Sarah paused for a second. "I think the drama wiped Anthony out. The two of them smelled disgusting when they got back. Anthony soaked in the tub while I hosed Hannibal until he was clean enough to come indoors. I'm cooking lamb shanks and gravy for them now, so I need to go. See you soon."

Patricia clicked off the phone. Friends had their own

lives, and she felt lonely. She did not think dogs sleeping with humans was hygienic, but tonight she invited Sophie onto the bed with her. Patricia kept one hand on her silky warmth as she prayed. *Dear Lord, I am afraid. Please help me.*

* * *

Even with earplugs in, the roar of motorcycles was terrifying, and Patricia sat bolt upright. Sophie jumped into her arms and burrowed beneath the quilt.

Through the gap in the bedroom curtains, Patricia counted twenty Harley motorcycles, each following the next at speed and skidding to a stop in front of the cottages. They wore black helmets and face masks. She recognized Darren when he took off his helmet and shouted a welcome to everyone. Headlights glinted off chains on their jackets. Girl passengers took off their helmets and shook out manes of long hair, screaming with laughter.

There was more engine noise from the back of the cottage. Quilt around her shoulders, Patricia crept onto the landing. People were parking one behind the other in the back lane and came up the path carrying bottles and cans. Someone shouted about Bonfire Night, and they piled all the packing boxes into the backyard and lit a bonfire. Someone threw gasoline on and a great spout of flame shot into the sky. People were drinking and having competitions with empty bottles, to hit things in her yard. Someone banged loudly on her front door.

Sophie was still under the bedcovers, and Patricia stood hesitantly at the top of the stairs. She saw the firecracker come through the letter slot. Hurrying down, she dropped the quilt over the handrail. The firecracker exploded and Patricia jumped down the rest of the stairs to stamp and extinguish the sparks. She picked up the quilt and wrapped it tightly around her again. Sitting on the bottom stair, she put a finger through one of the burned holes. Were they going to set the house on fire? If one firecracker had come through, would there be more? She waited, focused on the door, and heard the approaching sirens. Someone in the village had called the police.

Amid the flashing lights, shouting, tasers, and arrests, Patricia huddled in bed with Sophie. She waited for a knock on the door. But her cottage was in darkness and the police did not know she was there.

With the dawn, the last police car departed. Patricia felt like an animal afraid to leave its den but made herself dress in slacks and a warm sweater. She could not bear the bright lights of the kitchen, so gave Sophie her breakfast by the light from the hallway. She sat on a stool at the counter and ate cereal in slow motion. With the night's activities, Darren had emphasized his message. Next time, the punishment might be worse.

Patricia put the harness on Sophie and attached her leash. Wearing her red quilted coat, she opened the door and locked it again behind them. She guided Sophie through the trash, empty cans, and bottles to her front gate.

* * *

At St. Peter's, Patricia sat in the back pew and sank her head onto interlaced fingers. She was lost. Sophie slipped from beside her to greet someone, and Patricia looked up when Anthony sat down beside her. He put his arms out slowly, as if giving her the chance to refuse, but Patricia leaned toward him. He gently pulled her into an enormous bear hug. "You poor, poor girl. I walked Hannibal to the village early to get the newspaper and heard what happened."

Patricia's head was on Anthony's chest, and he held her

as if she was a small child. He whispered, "Can you tell me about it?"

He shifted her weight gently, so that her head rested in the curve of his neck. She breathed the scent of clean male skin and it quieted her panic. "Donna Smithers is the Tenant; the rest are family and groupies. I contacted the Citizens' Advice Bureau about evicting them, but they said I did not make the Tenancy Agreement specific enough. I must put up with them until their lease runs out."

Patricia gulped and sat up, searching for a tissue. Anthony found one in his pocket. "Thank you. They threatened us, and I need to find somewhere else to stay. Sophie and I are in danger and must move out."

Anthony sat back, and his face was anxious. "If you leave, they will break into your cottage and occupy it. At the end of the year, you will need bailiffs to evict them. They will trash everything before they disappear, and your insurance company will not pay for the damage."

Patricia's eyes widened. "How do you know?"

"I had a similar experience in London. You must go to the police. Why didn't you speak to an officer last night?"

"I was afraid to go out and have them see me. I watched who the police took away, and Darren is still at the cottage. Donna will be back."

Patricia pressed a hand to the ache in her chest. "Darren threatened to hurt Sophie and Donna would have hit me, but he stopped her. They will do whatever they want now, and I can never relax again."

Anthony took her hand in both of his. "Why don't you talk to Robert? He is an ex-police officer and your friend. My car is outside. I left Hannibal with Sarah so I could search for you. If you want, I can take you and Sophie to the Stables right now."

Chapter 14

Robert was in the top pony field, unloading hay from the Jeep. Patricia had texted from St. Peter's and he raised a hand in greeting as they bumped along the track to the gate. Anthony squeezed her hand. "I am going back to the Manor House to research some things and call our family lawyer in Oxford. Text me when you're ready and I will come back to get you."

"Thank you for being there, and for suggesting that I see Robert before I look at moving out."

Anthony's kind smile warmed her heart. "It's not you who needs to move out. These people are bullies and we will get your cottage back."

Patricia opened the big wooden gate so she and Sophie could slip through and close it again. Sophie ran out on her long leash to greet Robert and the ponies, her nose to their muzzles. Robert looked at Patricia's face and said, "I could do with a hand to finish here and then we can talk."

The ponies wore waterproof winter blankets, and some were lying down near the hedge. Tying Sophie's leash to the door of the Jeep, Patricia took an armful of hay wedges and followed him. She breathed clean air, and it felt reassuring to be among the ponies. When the hay rack was full, she brushed dust from her sleeves and Robert leaned against the Jeep. "A volunteer came in early and told me what happened at your cottage. Are you okay?"

Patricia shook her head. "No. I am scared. The man threatened to hurt Sophie if I go to the police."

Robert folded his arms across his chest. "Oh, I see, that sort, are they? I know officers in Woodstock and will drive you to file a complaint. They will add it to the report from last night. I called Clair and David after I got your text. They sent their love and said to bring you to the Stables meeting at noon."

Patricia bit her lip, and he pushed off the side of the Jeep to give her a hug. "Summerfield is a village and everyone knows everyone's business. This is getting out of hand and someone will get hurt. It horrified Clair that you have been alone in this and she suggested we brainstorm ideas to help you. We must work together as a team, like when we fought for the lease."

Robert opened the passenger door of the Jeep. "Come on, let's go to Woodstock and I will buy you a cup of coffee. We can go to the police station and be back in time for the meeting."

He gave Patricia a hand up into the passenger seat, and Sophie jumped in too. Robert climbed into the driver's seat. "David invited Anthony to the meeting. Apparently, he dealt with bad tenants in London and evicted them through a Tribunal."

Patricia fastened her seat belt and yawned. "Sorry. I am so tired."

Robert turned the Jeep in a big circle toward the gate and Patricia pointed, "What is that? There, next to Bonnie."

The ponies by the hedge were standing, all except for Bonnie, who was lying down. She was a sweet-tempered moorland pony, with a coat so thick she never needed a blanket. She was dozing, her eyes closed and muzzle resting on the ground. A black shape, like an enormous fallen blackbird, lay close against her side. Robert was approaching the gate, but he did not turn his head. "That is the boy from your cottage. He is often here during the day. I watch him with binoculars, and he does no harm, but he runs if he spots me. See how close he is to Bonnie? The others form a circle around them while they sleep."

Astonished, Patricia looked back. "They are on guard? Like an alert circle in the wild?"

Robert jumped out to open the gate. "It seems they have accepted him as one of the herd."

He jumped back in and drove through. "When I was an officer on street patrol, I saw a lot of homeless kids, but I've never seen one out here. How old is he? He only looks about fourteen."

Robert got back out to padlock the gate and when he climbed in again, Patricia said, "But he's not homeless, he lives with his family."

"It doesn't look like he gets much sleep there."

"We don't either." Sophie sat between Patricia's knees, leaning as they bumped along the track to the Oxford Road. "They play rap music at top volume all the time. I asked them to please turn it down. They slammed the door in my face and threatened us."

"Him too?" Robert gestured back toward the boy.

"No." Patricia remembered the strange glance that had passed between them. "I have never spoken to him. His mother, Donna, is the aggressive tenant and Darren is her partner."

She dropped her head and gulped. "Sarah told me I should have used an agency, and she was right. For someone who has lived sixty plus years, I am naïve."

Robert patted her hand. "We worried about you. But you normally manage everything so efficiently, and we didn't want to interfere."

Patricia was shamefaced. "Because I get prickly and offended? My son told me I am a perfectionist and don't like to get things wrong."

Robert laughed. "That too. But you try hard to make things perfect for everyone else, and you are a friend. Everyone makes mistakes. We call it being human."

* * *

At the police station, Robert found an officer he knew, who interviewed for a complaint against Donna Smithers. On the way back to the Stables meeting, Patricia shut her eyes. She was ashamed to be in a police file and dreaded the discussion ahead. She had been one of the team who met regularly to solve problems. This time, the problem was her.

Robert took Patricia into the Training Room and Clair rushed over to give her a hug. "Poor Patricia! How awful! We will help you, don't worry."

David patted her arm, "Things look bad, but hang in there."

Audrey leaned forward in her chair to pat Sophie and smile at Patricia, "I bet you haven't eaten. Can I make you a sandwich?"

"I would love one." Patricia felt humbled by the kindness of friends. Everyone sat down around the table and Anthony joined them. He was dressed in a business suit and carrying his laptop, smiling at Patricia as he took a seat—and a sandwich. "Thanks, Audrey."

David was the Chair of today's meeting. "We have several Stables items to discuss, but first, let's hear about Patricia's problem tenants."

Patricia held a tissue between sweaty hands. "Thank you, David. As you know, I am inexperienced at rental property. They fooled me into believing they were Christian and needed help. As soon as Donna got the keys, she showed her true personality. They have threatened me and Sophie."

A warm nose bumped Patricia's knee under the table, and she stroked the silky head as David turned to Anthony. "You said on the phone you have info on this woman?"

Anthony opened his laptop. "Confidentially, a legal friend revealed that Donna Smithers is a serial fraudster."

He read from the screen. "Donna Smithers left school at fifteen, never worked and has no tax records. She has eight children. The eldest ones, a daughter and son, live with her and the rest are in Council Care. She knows the legal system around tenancy and targets rookie landlords through publications like church magazines. She has been before Tenancy Tribunals in three counties."

Patricia leaned forward, and her eyes flashed. "She picks rookies like me and does this as a JOB?"

Anthony's face was sympathetic. "Afraid so. Halfmoon Cottages and your kindness were perfect for her purposes."

"But she had written references! I called them for confirmation."

"They were fraudulent. She would pay people to tell you whatever she wanted, to get the tenancy. Tribunal records are available to lawyers. Donna only pays the first month's rent. She stops on any excuse and gets eleven months free accommodation before the lease expires. She owes £9000 in unpaid rent and, in the Tribunal, offers to pay it back in small instalments; but she always defaults. When the debt reaches £10,000, she can declare bankruptcy and they wipe it clean."

Patricia was furious. "I grew up on a Council Housing estate. We were hard-working, ordinary people, like everyone else there. I have never met anyone like this, there or anywhere else."

David took a sip of his coffee and nodded sympathetically. "I hate to be cynical, but times have changed. Most people are decent, but there have always been rats."

"I have rats in the cottage next door." Patricia's face was glum. "The problem is, how do I get rid of them?"

Anthony cleared his throat. "There was an appointment available later this afternoon with our lawyer in Oxford and I booked it for you. Donna will only leave if you defeat her using the Law. I can cancel the appointment if you wish, but I'm happy to go with you and get the process started."

Patricia's face softened. "That is a great idea, and thank you for booking the appointment."

Anthony grinned. "I'm repaying a favor. Everyone here has heard about my adventures in the mud."

There were smiles around the table and David sniggered at his older brother as Anthony continued, "You stopped those cattle trampling me and Hannibal to death. If rats threaten you and Sophie, I will help get them evicted."

Clair looked relieved and stood to pour herself more coffee. "I am so glad you know a specialist, Anthony. I am going to call every evening from now on, Patricia, to check how you are."

Patricia smiled. "Thanks everyone. I'll go now and let you get on with Stables business."

She started to stand, but David raised a hand, "Just before that, my brother asked for a few minutes to share something personal with us."

Anthony's hands were in his lap, but he placed them, palms down, on the table in front of him. His right hand was perfectly still, but the little finger of the left hand danced a jig. It seemed unconnected to the rest of his hand and everyone, except David and Clair, looked shocked.

Anthony placed his right hand on the finger, and it was still. A moment later, he released it and the little finger continued its crazy jig. "I have Parkinson's disease."

Patricia's hand flew to her mouth, and he glanced at her. "It was a shock to me too. They diagnosed me two years ago. Drugs are effective in controlling Parkinson's, but I live in

Summerfield now and sometimes cannot mask the symptoms. I did not take my meds an hour ago, so you could see what happens."

Anthony looked around at their sympathetic eyes. "Patricia is bravely facing her demons. I want to do the same. It's a relief not to hide it any longer."

Chapter 15

Patricia and Anthony walked out to the white 4 x 4 in the Stables parking lot. "I need to wait another hour before the meds kick in and I can drive."

He held up the keys. "Are you okay? Shall I call a taxi?"

Patricia felt better from being with friends at the meeting, and she did not want Anthony calling Jim! She took the keys to the 4 x 4, and soon they joined a stream of traffic heading into Oxford. "Would you be comfortable telling me about Parkinson's disease? I know very little about it."

"I wish I knew nothing about it." Anthony looked out at the passing scenery and then back through the windshield. "In 1817, Dr. James Parkinson discovered that, without a chemical messenger called dopamine, the brain cannot control movement. Before that they called the condition *shaking palsy*, so I guess Parkinson's is a less gruesome label."

"Didn't Muhammad Ali, the boxer, have it? He lived to a good age, right?"

Anthony nodded. "He had Parkinson's for thirty-two years, was at the 2012 Olympic Games, and died at age seventy-four. Drugs control the symptoms, but there is no cure. I had a specialist in London, but he transferred me to the research unit at the Oxford hospital. I think Sarah guessed what I have, although she has never mentioned it. She just seems to take great care to stop me from getting too tired."

"Sarah originally trained as a nurse."

"I am glad it's out in the open and that you know too."

With Christmas approaching, there was no parking in central Oxford. They boarded a red double-decker bus in the Park 'n' Ride lot, and Anthony's voice was cheerful again. "However grim the situation, I am determined to make happy memories every day. Would you care to ride in the front seat on the top of the bus?"

* * *

Anthony greeted his friend at the law offices on St. Aldate's Street and introduced Patricia to him, then sat in the paneled waiting room with coffee. Patricia came out thirty minutes later looking more confident. "He was so helpful. I understand the eviction process better now and why they do not allow lawyers in the Tenancy Tribunal. But it is scary that I must represent myself. He is writing the first Warning Letter to Donna, and I need to come back at 4:00 p.m. to pick it up."

Anthony slid the laptop into his briefcase and closed the straps. "I read the file he put together on her. It is interesting that she has a conviction for assault."

Patricia raised an eyebrow as they walked out into the street. "Interesting? I wish I had known that when I went around there to challenge her. She could have beaten me up! However, because of that conviction, I am considered an at-risk client. The lawyer called the Court, and they gave me a priority place on the last Tribunal before Christmas. It is in ten days' time and I need to work fast. But he said that you knew the evidence needed from your London case."

Anthony nodded and looked at his watch, "Would you like tea somewhere, while we wait?"

Patricia breathed deeply. The anxiety of the past few days lessened as the streetlamps came on and glowing Christmas decorations brightened the dusky afternoon. "The Christmas Market on Broad Street opened today. This alleyway is a shortcut. Could we have something there?"

Anthony looked at the cobbles. "May I hold your arm? The meds are good now, but I don't want to trip."

His briefcase was in one hand and Patricia smiled as she took the other and tucked it through her arm. "It is always crowded at the Market, and there is nothing nicer than walking arm in arm with a friend. We can chat and look at everything, without losing each other."

The picture in the magazine at the medical center came into Patricia's mind as they strolled down the narrow lane and out into Broad Street. It was closed to vehicles, and the City Authorities had erected rows of Alpine chalets, covered in Christmas lights. There were lots of people warmly wrapped up in coats, hats, scarves, and gloves, sauntering along and buying from the stalls. Patricia sniffed appreciatively at the aroma of gingerbread. Every kind of locally made craft and homemade food was on display.

Anthony stopped at a stall selling Christmas wreaths of pinecones and dried fruits. Cinnamon, oranges, and honey spiced the air, and he held out his briefcase. "Could you please hold this for me for a minute?"

Patricia took it, smiling. She already had a festive wreath for her front door, so stood to one side and watched people. The little chalets were jolly, glowing with lights against the darkening sky. Behind a barrier of small Christmas trees, children of all ages, including seniors like herself, rode the Old Tyme Carousel! Exquisitely painted horses carried them as it rotated to the fairground music of a Wurlitzer organ. Patricia realized that she no longer felt hurt, thinking back to when she shared the Market with Charlotte and Amber, but suddenly, she startled at a face in the crowd. Surely that was not Jim?

Patricia had a sharp pang of guilt, like indigestion. She had not planned on coming to the Christmas Market with Anthony. She scanned the faces again and saw another man with a grey ponytail. Anthony held up a brushwood wheel, interwoven with pinecones, evergreens, dried red peppers, and citrus. "I like this one. What do you think?"

"Fabulous!"

He paid the smiling woman running the stall. "Thank you! Happy Holidays to you!"

Anthony was carrying a giant, brown bag with *Polly's Plantation* printed on it and offered it to Patricia in exchange for the heavier briefcase. "Last year, our family met in a London hotel and bought gifts online. This is the first time I have been Christmas shopping in years!"

They walked on and Patricia happily swung the Christmas wreath in its bag. Anthony took her arm again. "This year, Sarah will decorate the Manor House for me. David and Clair are coming for a Christmas dinner one night. Would you join us?"

"I would love to."

Anthony paused at an Alpine bar selling mulled wine. "I called Sarah while you were with the lawyer. She sent her love and suggested I ask you and Sophie back to dinner. "Would you like a mulled wine now? I will have a coffee."

"How lovely that Sarah is cooking dinner! I would like to go get Sophie and the car, and I will drive back to Summerfield this time, so I'll join you in a coffee, please."

The red-and-white Swiss flags waved on flexible stalks from the stall as they sat down at a little metal table. Coffee was served in hand-painted pottery mugs and Anthony sipped. "Ah, that is good! I hate drinking out of plastic cups. He leaned back in his chair, watching people passing. "I was thinking, my vehicle is bigger than yours, could I help you collect or deliver food for the Food Bank?"

Patricia warmed her hands around her coffee mug and understood that he was trying to make amends. "That would be splendid, thank you."

He turned serious brown eyes to her. "You won't abandon me and Hannibal to walk alone? I cannot tell you how much I enjoy your company on our walks."

Patricia gently clinked her mug against his. "The walks are on again. Do you think we could ride the carousel before we go get the letter and head home?"

* * *

People poured off the carousel when the music stopped. It was nearly dark as Patricia climbed onto a beautiful blue-and-gold horse with *Darcy* written on its neck. The ride filled quickly, so Anthony took the second seat behind her. He slid an arm around either side and held the striped pole below her hands. Patricia felt the tickle of his beard as he laughed in her ear. "Hold tight!"

The Market lights blurred into ribbons of red, white, and green. *Darcy* sprang into the air and sank again to the glorious *Oh, what a Beautiful Morning*, from the musical, *Oklahoma*. Anthony sang and Patricia joined in, closing her eyes. It was magic. Anthony held her safe, and she remembered being a little girl on her first carousel ride. Then the ride slowed. Patricia sighed and opened her eyes. Above the heads of the crowd, she made eye contact with Jim.

They dismounted from the carousel and returned to the lawyer's office to pick up the letter. On the bus to the Park 'n' Ride and driving home, she thought she would tell Anthony about Jim, but decided against it. Hopefully, she could explain to Jim when she saw him next. For now, the letter for Donna burned in her purse, demanding her attention. She must steel herself to deliver it tomorrow.

Anthony turned on the interior light and took a small microphone from his briefcase. He clipped it underneath his collar, threading long wires under his jacket and attaching them to a miniature recording device. Patricia glanced briefly sideways as she drove. "What is that for?"

"I brought it along on the off chance we might use it. I needed recorded evidence to get the London tenants evicted. Testing, testing."

Anthony played the recording back and slid the small black box into the pocket of his overcoat. "How about, we go get Sophie, take your Morris, and leave the 4 x4 at the Stables until morning? I can drive it back when I walk Hannibal tomorrow. You have only a short lead time before the Tribunal and need to start the process by giving Donna the first Warning letter tonight."

Patricia's hands tightened on the steering wheel. "Oh, what a terrible end to a happy afternoon!"

"I will be nearby and record what she says. You need evidence on the parking nuisance. You should state again that the space outside Halfmoon Cottages is a no parking area."

* * *

Donna opened the front door to Patricia's knock. Loud music thundered all around her and she shouted over her shoulder, "TURN IT OFF!"

Surprisingly, somebody did.

"You again!"

Patricia thrust the letter into her hands and Donna's face became ugly when she recognized it. Then she laughed, ripped open the envelope and read a few words.

She ripped the letter up and threw it into the air. Pieces

fluttered around them like snow as she thrust her face at Patricia. "I am sick of neurotic old women, rolling in money and owning houses, weeping and wailing about how badly I treat them."

She put her hands on her hips and scoffed. "You poor old thing, spending all that money on a lawyer. I reckoned you would do this, so it is your own fault that I have canceled the rent. You don't stand a chance! I've won more Tenancy Tribunals than you've had hot dinners."

Patricia held steady eye contact and Donna cackled, "They don't evict mothers with babies, especially just before Christmas. Then you won't get another chance for six months."

"Mrs. Smithers," Patricia spoke clearly for the recording. "I have asked you twice not to park in front of Halfmoon Cottages. It is a no parking area and I am telling you for the third time, you must not park there. As the tenant, you are also responsible that other vehicles do not park there."

Donna narrowed her eyes and let rip with a string of threats. Anthony stepped from the dark and stood beside Patricia. Donna stopped mid-syllable. She looked him up and down then shrieked with laughter. "Is this your body-guard? Oh dear, so old and bald! I am not impressed."

Anthony turned Patricia back down the path and Donna's voice followed them. "Forget the Eviction Order. We are staying right here and you ain't seen nothing yet!"

* * *

Patricia climbed wearily into the Morris and hugged a tail-wagging Sophie. Anthony sat in the passenger seat and disconnected the microphone, "What a piece of work that woman is! You did well to stay calm."

"I would have been scared on my own, but I coped, knowing that you were near."

Anthony re-played the recording. '*Is this your body-guard? Oh dear, so old and bald! I am not impressed.*'

Anthony clicked OFF and grinned at Patricia. "I could take exception to that. Officially, they classify my hair as receding."

He packed everything away into his briefcase. "The recording prints with the date and now we have evidence of her threatening you. You can have the Second Written Warning letter delivered tomorrow by courier, and it is Strike One against Mrs. Smithers. Let's go, Sarah is waiting dinner for us!"

Chapter 16

At the Manor House, Anthony and Patricia fed the dogs and sat down to dinner with Sarah in the kitchen. Patricia relaxed among friends and was glad she had faced Donna. Sarah served homemade cottage pie with fresh vegetables and Anthony tilted his head back, breathing in the aroma. "That smells so good, coming home on a chilly winter's night, and thanks for suggesting we eat here; the dining room is too formal."

Patricia took the plate Sarah passed to her. "This looks lovely. Just what I need for courage. I am dreading going back to the cottage and another night with no sleep."

Sarah sat down with her own meal. "I am glad things went so well with the lawyer." They ate quietly for a few minutes, then Sarah looked at Patricia with crinkled forehead and said, "I am upset you did not tell me what was happening. I could have at least shared your misery."

Patricia looked down at her plate, "I was ashamed. You told me I should have used an agency, and you were right. But I forged ahead, being a *do-gooder* and not thinking it through. You have every right to say, I told you so."

"You really thought I would say that?" Sarah laid a reassuring hand on Patricia's arm. "Sometimes things do not go to plan and friends still help, even if it was your own fault."

Patricia laughed ruefully. "I am still working on trying to not be perfect all the time. Growing up at home, if we made a mess, we cleared it up. I became desperate because I could not clear this up on my own."

Anthony sat back, hands folded across his contented tummy, seeming deep in thought. Patricia and Sarah finished eating, and he leaned forward again, "The Tribunal is in ten days and your request for an Eviction Order will only be successful with watertight evidence."

Sarah brought a deep-dish apple crumble to the table while he and Patricia cleared dishes into the dishwasher. "I am worried about what Donna will do to stop me now that she knows my intention."

Sarah served the dessert. "I would be nervous too. Sophie cannot even bark to warn you. But Hannibal is more confident now and knows you; if you cannot move out, could he stay at your cottage and guard you?"

Patricia lifted a spoonful of apple and ice cream, shaking her head. "Unfortunately, it does not work like that. Dogs form bonds. They only risk injury to defend family members."

Anthony nodded his agreement. "Until I got a dog of my own, I thought they were mobile defense units! Hannibal is still bonding with me. Much as I want to help, I cannot lend him to anyone else."

Hearing his name, Hannibal came to Anthony, who patted and praised him. Sarah looked at the two of them, then at Patricia. "You have two bedrooms and two bathrooms in your cottage. Could Hannibal and Anthony both stay with you until the Tribunal?"

Anthony looked up as he gently pulled Hannibal's ears. "That would be fine with the monster dog and me."

Patricia chewed her lower lip, tempted to say yes immediately. "I would feel so much safer, but what will people say?"

Sarah jumped up to give her a hug. "People will gossip

anyway, and that woman thinks she can bully you. You are in real danger and we will help you fight back."

Anthony grinned at Patricia. "Sarah is right. Hannibal and I would love to come and stay."

* * *

Anthony packed while Patricia drove Sarah to get the 4 x 4. Back at the Manor House, they loaded up and Sarah drove them to Halfmoon Cottages. "You could leave both cars with me at the Manor House, in case of 'accidental' damage by your tenants in St. Peter's parking lot. I can drive you places."

Patricia leaned from the back of the car, wedged between Hannibal's crate and boxes, with Sophie on her lap. "That is a great idea, and I need to find a security guard for when we are away from the cottage. The lawyer said the police suspected Donna and Co. of setting a tenancy house on fire. We can't risk the dogs being left alone in the cottage."

Anthony called Ecclesiastical Security, the company that guards St. Peter's, while Sarah parked behind Donna's car. They began unloading and Donna came to her front gate. "We are going out now and you need to move."

Patricia waved cheerily, "No worries, we won't be long."

She continued into Number 1 with Hannibal's giant dog bed. A security van pulled up behind the 4 x 4 and Anthony went to meet the two guards. He brought them into the kitchen to introduce them to Patricia and Sarah. Everyone shook hands and sat down around the table with tea and cookies. Someone pounded on the front door and Anthony smiled at Patricia, "Would you like Hannibal and I to answer that?"

He soon came back and thirty minutes later, Patricia signed the contract and shook hands with the security guys.

"Thanks for the tea. It was nice meeting you. We will monitor everything now and text regular updates to you."

"I'm off too." Sarah hugged Patricia and patted the dogs. "Call me if you need anything."

Patricia opened the front door and behind her, heard Sarah quietly ask Anthony, "Do you have all your meds?"

Waving goodbye, they were like two friends with two dogs going on a camping trip. Anthony picked up his small bag to follow Patricia upstairs. "Where shall Hannibal and I pitch our tent?"

They saw Donna's car reverse along Church Lane as she showed him to the second bedroom, "No earplugs tonight! You can have this bathroom, and I will shower downstairs."

When they returned to the kitchen, Sophie was curled up in Hannibal's giant bed and he stood glumly next to her.

"Sophie!"

Anthony laughed. "Leave them be. They will sort it out."

Hannibal gave a sigh and lay down on Sophie's medium-sized dog bed, with most of him on the floor. His broad, battered face rested among Sophie's cuddly toys, and Patricia took a photo to send to Sarah.

Look at Hannibal! So cute!
    I have a visit with Ted booked for tomorrow morning. Will walk to you and get the Morris after that.
        We need another giant dog bed!

When Patricia climbed into bed later, she noticed the quiet. It was heavenly without the neighbors—until Anthony and Hannibal started snoring in unison!

Patricia sat up to put in earplugs and leaned down to pat Sophie in her normal bed beside her. "Snoring is a small price to pay for having our own guardian angels staying here."

* * *

She slept well and enjoyed a relaxed breakfast with Anthony. "I can clear the dishes if you are visiting Ted."

Patricia gave him a spare set of keys for the cottage. There was no sound from next door and neither the motorcycle nor Donna's car were there when she and Sophie set out to walk to the Stables.

Marching along, warm in her red coat and gloves, she thought about Anthony. It was strange to have a man staying with her after all this time alone. But it was Anthony, and it felt like they had been friends forever. She glanced at her watch and speeded up. "Come on Sophie, I want to see Clair while Ted's caregivers are with him."

At Stables Cottage, she peeled off her coat and hung it up before letting Jossie into the yard with Sophie. Clair arrived from the stable yard and hugged Patricia. "Oh my, the village was buzzing about the burglaries around Summerfield. But now all the talk is of the nice verger who has become a scarlet woman!"

"Oh, don't!" Patricia put her hand on her heart. She had told Clair everything when she called last night. "I am so embarrassed. Ted doesn't know, does he?"

Patricia sat down at the kitchen table as Clair poured coffee. "Granddad is sleeping a lot and not even watching TV. He seems happiest looking at his photo book."

She rested her feet in striped boot socks on the bottom bar of the Aga stove. "He eats nothing at all, but the District Nurse says he is doing fine, as long as he drinks lots of water. She brought him an oxygen tank and the caregivers are fantastic. David and I could not manage our jobs without them."

A young woman in a lavender scrubs uniform came out of Ted's room, and Clair walked to the front door with her, discussing calendars, meds, and care. Patricia took her coffee and tapped on Ted's door. "It's Patricia, may I come in?"

She peeped around and Ted smiled to see her. The caregiver had angled him on white pillows and buttoned his green pajamas to the top. Patricia gave him a kiss and he smelled of baby powder. "How are you doing?"

He seemed brighter than last time, and she sat down next to the bed. "Did Clair tell you what Robert has been up to?"

Patricia was grateful Ted did not know what she had been up to! "Tell me."

"You know our two black horses, Blackbird and Rebel?"

She nodded and sipped her coffee. It was good to see Ted's eyes shining, as they always did when he talked about horses.

"Last year, me and Robert had a drink in the Potlatch with the funeral director. I talked about them originally being carriage horses. He told me he was restoring a horse-drawn Victorian hearse. Robert says he has completed it and wants Blackbird and Rebel to pull it for special funerals."

"So that is why he was in the lane, practicing with a long cart."

Ted reached for the oxygen mask. He waved Patricia away when she went to help, so she went to the window and watched Sophie and Jossie. After a few minutes, Ted removed the mask. "Robert enjoys driving. We agreed. He can use those horses for special funerals and when my time comes, he will take me to St. Peter's in that coach!"

Exhausted with the effort of speaking, Ted's eyes closed, and he slept. Patricia gazed at his face, changing, just as her parents had changed. His skin was transparent and blue veins stood out on his forehead. Mum, Dad and Ron had gone into hospice care, but she was glad Ted had community support at home. Patricia rested her hands in her lap and shut her eyes.

Dear Lord, please look after Ted.
Look after Clair and David when he dies.
And guide me to support, not disempower.

Patricia had grieved Ron's passing, but they had married young and in later years, settled into a pattern of marriage. They had Paul, their home, and jobs. Life had been okay, but she liked being free. Being married again did not appeal to her, and she prayed for a continuing friendship with Anthony.

Ted opened his eyes. "Could you pass my photo book to me, please?"

Patricia laid it in his hands, and it opened to his wedding pictures. Ted gently touched May's face in the sepia photograph. "You said you would read that bit for me, about a time to be born and a time to die?"

Patricia reached into her bag for her Bible.

"Ecclesiastes 3.

To everything there is a season, and a time to every purpose under heaven:

A time to plant, and a time to pluck up that which is planted.

A time to kill, and a time to heal; a time to break down, and a time to build up.

A time to weep, and a time to laugh; a time to mourn, and a time to dance.

A time to cast away stones, and a time to gather stones together,

A time to embrace, and a time to refrain from embracing.

A time to get, and a time to lose; a time to keep, and a time to cast away.

A time to rend, and a time to sew; a time to keep silence, and a time to speak.

A time to love, and a time to hate, a time of war, and a time of peace.

A time to be born, and a time to die.

Ted repeated the words. "A time to be born, and a time to die. All Clair's family died too soon. May and me, we were born again with the precious gift of that little girl. Would you help her when the time comes?"

Patricia took his hand and squeezed it gently. "You know that I will."

Ted lay on his pillows, the corners of his eyes wet. "I'm weary, dear. I'm ready to go, when the good Lord sees fit to take me."

He slept again and Patricia's sight blurred as she held his work-roughened hand. Tears fell for a dear friend and for her own mortality.

Chapter 17

Patricia walked Sophie from Stables Cottage to the Manor House to get her car and went to the pet store in Banbury. Back home, walking along Church Lane and carrying a new giant dog bed, Patricia heard music. It was not rap! She danced a few steps as she rounded the bend, *"The corn is as high as an elephant's eye…"*

It was 1950s Broadway and delightfully familiar. Patricia smiled sweetly up at Donna, grimacing from the upper window of Number 2, and opened her front door. The volume was appalling, even for Rogers and Hammerstein! Anthony hurried from the kitchen with earplugs and Patricia put them in with a sigh of relief. Sophie jumped around with Hannibal and she let them out the back door. A pad and pen lay on the countertop and Anthony wrote on it.

How is Ted?

Patricia took the pen and wrote back.

Sleepy but good. Where did this amazing sound system come from?
    Rap rats returned and very noisy. Had big parties in the courtyard of London apartment. Got Sarah to bring speakers from Manor House.

Patricia's delight showed as she wrote.

Yay! You are seriously upsetting Donna!

How could it be fun when the situation was so dire? Patricia washed her hands and made vegetable soup. Her heart was lighter as Anthony played with his techie stuff and wrote on the pad again.

Will put on automatic loop when we go to bed… any requests?
    1812 Overture? Handel's Messiah?

She set the table for lunch and Anthony unloaded the dishwasher. With earplugs in, Patricia felt, rather than heard, the big china bowl crash to the floor. He and he stared at his hands in frustration and the scrawl on the pad was shaky.

Sometimes can't coordinate… will replace.
    No worries.

Anthony went to the laundry room to get the dustpan and Patricia put bowls of soup onto the table. Through the sitting room window, she saw Tracey and Donna load the baby and stroller into the car. They reversed up Church Lane. Anthony switched off the sound system, and they took out their earplugs. Patricia passed him the breadbasket. "What a relief! My stomach is so tense when they are around that I get indigestion. This afternoon, I shall have the luxury of digging in the yard, with only the sound of birds to accompany me."

"While I sit on the patio, watch you work, and read the newspaper!" They both laughed.

Wearing old gardening clothes, Patricia enjoyed working the vegetable patch, ready for spring planting. It was chilly, but the clouds parted now and again to reveal blue sky. Warm in his coat and stockman hat, Anthony sat on a patio chair with *The Times* spread on the table. To one side, finches, robins, and tiny wrens visited the bird feeder. Sophie watched them with a warning from Patricia.

Eventually, Sophie got bored and trotted down the path. Hannibal galloped after her but this time, when he bounced on her, she was ready. Her teeth snapped on his nose and Hannibal yelped. He turned to run but was no match for a furious white-and-black tornado, who nipped him everywhere. The two dogs sped down the path, Hannibal weaving to avoid her, his tail between his legs. Patricia grinned at Anthony. "I guess he won't be bouncing on her again for a bit!"

Sophie returned and went indoors. Hannibal snuck back and sat close to Anthony, who stroked his head. "Poor old fella. Better learn who is really *the Boss*."

He found a chewie strip in his coat pocket, and Hannibal lay down to gnaw. He was a fast eater. Patricia moved away from the newly turned earth; he was still full of energy and leaped into the vegetable patch, to dig furiously. Anchoring his newspaper with one hand, Anthony looked at Patricia, "Shall I stop him?"

She shook her head. "Nothing is planted yet."

They watched Hannibal for several minutes. He threw back the earth until he could splay out his front paws and drop his head into the hole. Here, he froze, with his rump stuck in the air. Patricia laughed. "What is he doing?"

Anthony folded the newspaper. "I thought he was listening for moles, but David says it is a behavior from Afghanistan. They trained Hannibal to listen for ticking."

The big dog shook the dirt from his coat and Patricia patted him, "Old habits die hard, don't they?"

Anthony filled in the hole. "If you have white paint and brushes left from decorating, we could paint a NO PARKING sign across the whole space in front of the cottages. She will park on it anyway, but you can take dated photographs as another piece of evidence for the Tribunal."

"Good thinking. Let's do it, then take the dogs for a long walk."

Patricia stayed in her gardening clothes. She found white paint, disposable gloves, and two paintbrushes. Anthony changed into old clothes and put the dogs into a *down* position in the front yard. "Stay! We will take you in a little while."

He drew the outlines of enormous letters and they had painted half before the door of Number 2 opened. Darren marched down the path. "Stop that! I know what you are up to."

He surprised Patricia. The motorcycle was there, but the silence had made her think he was not. Darren came storming through the gate and reached to grab Anthony's paintbrush. There was a snarl, like that of an angry bear and Darren turned, arm upraised over Anthony. The enormous dog rose from the bushes and paced forward on his toes. All his black hair stood on end, revealing gruesome, white scars. His eyes were fixed on Darren and an ominous growl rumbled deep in his throat. Hannibal lifted his upper lip and the light gleamed off massive white fangs.

"Good dog, stay."

Hannibal stood motionless as Darren dropped his arm and backed up the path. He tried to shout but stuttered, "That's a dangerous dog. I'll report you to the police."

He slammed the front door and Anthony squatted beside Hannibal to smooth his fur. "You are a good boy and listening well."

Hannibal licked Anthony's hand as he gave both dogs a treat. He and Patricia continued painting. When they completed the last letter, Anthony replaced the lid on the paint can. "Tomorrow, you can take photos of Donna's car parked here, then call the lawyer to send the Final Warning letter."

Patricia went upstairs to change for their walk and checked another item off her list.

* * *

The walk in Potlatch Wood was a joyful release. They enjoyed the nip in the air and rustle of leaves underfoot. When they got home, Patricia lit the sitting room fire and Sophie settled into Hannibal's bed. It had a dark plaid cover, so Patricia had bought blue denim for Sophie. With a sigh, Hannibal climbed into her bed and Anthony commiserated. "It's the same size, buddy, so no hardship."

He put spaghetti into a pan of boiling water, adding a little salt and olive oil. Headlights showed at the sitting room window as Donna parked. It was too dark for photos. Within minutes, the heavy beat pounded through the wall and Patricia shrugged as she stirred her bolognaise sauce. "Earplug time!"

Making dinner with Anthony was nice, but she suddenly felt anxious. Were they getting too close?

She pushed the thought away and finished the sauce with chopped oregano. Anthony laid plates, napkins, and silverware. He lit the candles, and the table looked romantic. Patricia wrote on the pad.

Beautiful! Are you ready to eat now?

He drew a smiley face emoji, poured water for them both, and a glass of wine for Patricia.

They had just served the food and were about to eat when headlights appeared in the back lane. Anthony jumped to his feet and turned off the lights. Drawing the kitchen blinds, he took out his earplugs and shouted, "Quick, close the drapes in the sitting room and put up the fireplace screen."

Startled, Patricia did as he said. She covered their dinners with saucepan lids and blew out the candles. She went to stand next to him and peer between the kitchen blinds. "What is happening? Hannibal, shh! Sophie, stay."

Anthony leaned close as people came up the path next door. "Can you go into the bathroom and call the police on the number they gave you? Tell them what is happening. We will take our dinner upstairs and watch the show!"

Twenty minutes later, Patricia and Anthony sat in the landing window with their dinner on trays. Music still pounded, more people arrived and then came the shriek of sirens. Police cruisers swept into both the front and rear of the cottages. Officers with police sniffer dogs came through the backyard and people ran out the front. Anthony finished his dinner. "Delicious!"

The police arrested Darren and two other men, but not Donna or Tracey. There was no sign of Tracey's boyfriend or Goth Boy, but an officer carried out a set of pharmacy scales and small white bags. Patricia was enjoying her wine and suddenly pointed. "Look!"

Officers carried televisions and home entertainment units to the trunk of a police cruiser. "They must be from the burglaries!"

In the revolving orange light of the patrol cars, Anthony's face was jubilant. "Strike Two! All Tenancy Agreements specify that tenants do not use the property for illegal purposes. As the owner of the cottage, you can get a copy of the police report. Donna has categorically broken the Tenancy Agreement!"

When all the cars had gone, they took their trays downstairs and the music did not start again. Anthony let the dogs out while Patricia took a shower. She let them in again, checked the doors, turned off the lights, and followed them upstairs. Anthony crossed the landing to his room, wearing a beige robe. Patricia self-consciously tightened the belt of the pink bathrobe that covered her from neck to furry slippers. "I am still puzzled. How did the police know it was drugs?"

Anthony threw his head back and guffawed. "What I love most about you is your innocence! Everybody knows that sports shoes thrown over power lines means drugs are for sale there."

Patricia was indignant. "Everybody does *not* know that! *I* did not know—and there goes the last scrap of my reputation! How am I going to live that one down?"

Chapter 18

"Hallelujah!"

On Sunday morning, after the drugs raid, Anthony began the day with the *Hallelujah Chorus* from Handel's *Messiah*.

Patricia's church in Oxford had staged a performance several years before and she knew all the words. It was exhilarating to play glorious music at enormous volume but hear it normally through earplugs. The dogs were outside to avoid damage to their hearing, but Patricia sang joyfully at the top of her voice.

Wintery sun broke through the mist and glittered on the frosty grass. Hannibal came racing toward the deck, barking, and the furious face of Donna Smithers appeared at the top of the fence. Patricia guessed she must be standing on a patio chair. Patricia asked Anthony to mute the music, took out her earplugs and opened the door. "Mrs. Smithers. I gather you dislike my music as much as I dislike yours. We have measured the decibels with a phone app. Every night that you disturb our sleep, we will enjoy our music early in the morning, at the same decibel level. When you are considerate, we will be too."

Patricia brought the dogs in, closed the door, and put

her earplugs in again. Anthony wound up the volume, and mouthing obscenities, Donna disappeared. Patricia wrote on the pad.

THANK YOU so much for helping me regain my sense of humor! It is quietest in my bedroom, so I will shut the dogs in there with water, until we get back from St. Mary's.

Anthony did a thumbs up and Patricia took Sophie and Hannibal upstairs while she changed for church. Blessed Sunday, the second of Advent and only three weeks till Christmas.

When Patricia came down again, Anthony had made a loop of canned Christmas supermarket music. She locked the front door behind them, and he clicked the remote. *Jingle Bells* filled the wintery morning air around the cottages, as loud and cheerful as the Mall on a Christmas Saturday.

Patricia found the bass beat very pleasing. "How jolly! One of Santa's elves will peep from behind a tree at any minute! How many times will they be treated to this loop before we get back?"

Anthony calculated as they walked along Church Lane. "Umm, nineteen, possibly twenty times?"

"Lovely!"

* * *

Sarah waited for them in the white 4 x 4 and Patricia waved as a white van drew up next to her. *Ecclesiastical Security* was painted on its sides and the guard had drunk tea with them that first evening. "I am on my way to the cottages now."

Patricia smiled and handed him a box of earplugs. Less anxious, now that he was on duty, she climbed into the back of the 4 x 4. "Hi! Thanks for picking us up. It is fabulous to be out of the house, and I am looking forward to Tim's sermon."

The 9:00 a.m. choir practice was fun and focused on the upcoming Christmas program. Anthony was firmly coached to stop dominating with his strong bass voice, and Patricia sympathized. "You were singing at cottage decibel level!"

Coffee break was with Audrey and choir friends, where all the talk was of the drugs raid. Everyone quieted as they prepared for service, buttoning dark-blue robes, and pulling on starched, white surplices over them. The verger of St. Mary's led them into the church, his ceremonial staff topped with the symbol of the crossed keys. The congregation stood as they entered in pairs and proceeded down the central aisle. Reaching her place in the choir stalls, Patricia breathed in the clean scent of Advent evergreens. Tim entered, dressed in his purple Advent robes.

They sang the opening hymn and there were prayers. Tim bounded up the pulpit steps. "Christmas approaches, thanks be to God!"

He beamed down at them, his glasses glinting. "Last week, our visiting minister from Uganda told us about Christmas in his parish. Today, I will eat chocolate and speak of Advent."

He held up a modern Advent Calendar with twenty-four little windows. He opened one and ate the chocolate. There were shouts and laughter from the children. "Um, nice, but insignificant."

He put it aside and held up his Bible. "That Advent calendar was invented in 1900. The Christian Advent Calendar has heralded Christmas for two thousand years."

He pushed the glasses up on his nose. "The word *Advent* means arrival and proclaims the coming of a miraculous baby, bringing hope to a troubled world."

His face grew serious. "Believe me, they had troubles in the time of Jesus too. Roman military occupation and persecution. Joseph had to take Mary on a long journey to Bethlehem to pay his taxes. For us, every day brings updates on war, terrorism, and disaster all over the world. To survive and thrive, we must hold on to love and the true meaning of Christmas."

He pointed to the table which held an Advent wreath, with one purple candle lit." Each Sunday for the four weeks before Christmas, we light a candle. The first three are purple for repentance. We prepare for the arrival with regret for the things we have done wrong. We determine not to repeat our mistakes."

A member of the Youth Church came forward to light the second purple candle and Tim smiled his thanks. "On the Fourth Sunday before Christmas, we light the rose candle, to signify the joy to come. At midnight on Christmas Eve, the lighted, white candle celebrates the arrival of Jesus, the Light of the World."

Tim looked happy. But then leaned over the pulpit and asked the congregation, "How will we celebrate this miraculous gift? With sacred music, feasting with family and friends, plus some earthly gifts, we hope! But will we also share with the poor, the homeless, and the lonely? In the spirit of Christmas, will we reach out to our neighbors?"

In the choir stalls opposite, Anthony's eyes held Patricia's and twinkled at her. She had been thinking about Food Bank gift baskets. His grin reminded her of how they were reaching out to their neighbors, with the gift of sacred music. She looked away quickly before she grinned back at him. Patricia repented that she had been arrogant and not worked harder to understand Donna's background. Was there anything she could do to help her now?

* * *

Sarah gave Anthony a white grocery bag when she dropped them at St. Peter's. "I got everything you asked for."

Patricia sang along with *I'm Dreaming of a White Christmas* as they walked back to the cottage. The guard waved as he backed his van along the lane, and they squeezed past Donna's car into their front yard. Hannibal barked and Anthony turned off the sound system. There was an unaccustomed silence from next door as Patricia let the dogs into the backyard. "I am going to change and take photos of Donna's car. Are cold cuts, jacket potatoes, and salad okay for lunch?"

"Great! I am cooking a special dinner for you tonight."

Anthony opened the silverware drawer to set the table, but the knives and forks exploded from his hands. He sighed; his face frustrated as he looked at the scattered silverware. "I need to take a tablet and will be back to pick those up."

He slowly climbed the stairs. Patricia poured herself a glass of tonic water and sat down to watch the dogs. If she picked anything up it would make it worse for Anthony. Hannibal was digging again but had not bounced on Sophie since she taught him that lesson.

Setting boundaries in a new relationship?

Patricia sipped her tonic water and mulled over how well she set boundaries with some people and how badly with others. She had probably caused the problems with Paul and Eve. She let things build up without setting clear boundaries, then got resentful when people took advantage. And what was going to happen with her and Anthony when all this was over?

* * *

After a pleasant lunch, they walked the dogs and Anthony said he felt better. "The plumbers are coming tomorrow to give a quote for replacing the heating pipes at St. Peter's, and I want to check a few things. I won't be long. Come, Hannibal."

Patricia sat on Ted's family bench with Sophie and enjoyed the winter sunshine. A dark figure stepped from the shadow of the yew trees and startled them. Jim wore his taxi driving clothes. His hands were curled into fists by his sides and his face was an angry red, as he hissed at her, "I saw you at the Christmas Market! You saw me too, so don't pretend you didn't."

Patricia stood and put her hand on Sophie's head, her eyes on Jim's as he ranted at her,

"You rented that cottage to trashy people, not even asking if anyone in the village wanted to rent it. Summerfield never heard a police siren before this. Now the village has a reputation for burglaries, motorcycle gangs, drugs, and police raids. There are strange kids hanging around the War Memorial, and parents are keeping our youngsters indoors. And it's all your fault."

Jim breathed hard, "You say no to a date with an honest, hard-working man, but you let the Lord of the Manor move in!"

"Come, Sophie." Patricia walked toward the church, her back stiff. It was all true, but she did not need this right now. She could not explain to a jealous man who was unlikely to listen. Jim did not follow but shouted after her, "The last verger was worthy of respect! You are a disgrace to St. Peter's!"

Patricia shut the church door and depression swept over her. Hannibal trotted over to greet Sophie and Anthony came out of the robing room. "It's all good for tomorrow. I will come over early and… "

He hurried up the aisle. "What happened? Is Donna out there?"

Patricia sat down in the nearest pew. "Not Donna; Jim."

Anthony sat down next to her. She told him about Ted's warning, Jim asking for a date and seeing them together on the carousel. Patricia dropped her head, hating to repeat the words. "He said everyone knows you are living with me and that I am a disgrace to St. Peter's."

Anthony laughed and squeezed her hand. "I am sorry to laugh, dear, but I'm glad I got the carousel ride with you and not Jim. He wanted to hurt you by saying that. and we know the truth. So does everyone else who cares about you. When the Tenancy Tribunal is over, the village will talk about that too."

He pulled out his key ring. "To put everything in perspective, today is the day we climb the tower!"

"But Tim said the tower is unsafe."

"Only if you stand up. There is a ledge with a low wall around it at the bottom of the steeple. It is safe to sit there and we did it with the verger when we were choir boys. "He pulled Patricia to her feet. "The sun is out; I will shut the dogs in the robing room, and dare you to climb St. Peter's Tower with me."

* * *

The sign on the small door read:

Do not enter the tower, unless accompanied by the verger.

"That's you!" Anthony grinned, and handed her a key. "This one belongs on your keyring now."

Patricia unlocked the door and looked up the narrow spiral staircase. It smelled of cold stone and dust. Anthony took her hand and placed it on a thick dusty rope that ran through metal hoops in the wall. "You go first. I can catch you if you fall backward."

Patricia wanted to say, *What about you with Parkinson's? What if you fall backward?*

But she said nothing. She began to climb and with frequent stops to pant, they counted eighty steps to the trapdoor. Anthony slid the bolt, and sunshine flooded in as he flipped the trapdoor open. He moved carefully to sit on the ledge and wedged his feet against the low wall, before offering Patricia his hand.

What was she doing?

Only a short while ago she had threatened to resign because of this man. Now she was doing a dangerous thing, going up the tower with him!

Equally carefully, she settled on the ledge in the sunshine and they gazed out over the countryside. "Oh, wow!"

Past the drop off at the edge of the roof, the view was stupendous. Bright blue sky stretched to the horizon, with pale winter clouds gathering in the distance. Below them, rich agricultural land was a patchwork of sepia woods and brown, plowed fields. The farmhouses, cattle, and sheep looked like wooden toys you could reach down and pick up. Patricia still held Anthony's hand. "I would never have done this without you."

In answer, he raised her hand to his lips and kissed it. Sunlight rippled between them as Patricia looked at his brown eyes and kind mouth. She had never been kissed by a man with a beard before. Anthony gently traced her cheekbone with a fingertip, and she closed her eyes. He kissed tentatively, like a teenage boy. But the arms around her were strong and manly.

His lips brushed her neck as he whispered, "As soon as the Tribunal is over, I need to go to Kalamata. You have been under great strain. Would you like to come with me and have a little vacation?"

They held each other and Anthony did not rush her; he was tender and in control. Patricia relaxed in the high air and the sunshine. "It is a kind thought. But why are you going to Kalamata? Where is it? I have never heard of it before."

Anthony sat close, his arm about her waist. "My father, Sir George, lives permanently on his yacht in the Mediterranean. He is eighty-seven and his caregiver is twenty. The Captain called me because Dad asked him to marry them."

Anthony laughed. "Long story, short version... this is the second time Dad has done this, but with a different caregiver. I hold Power of Attorney and the Captain needs me to sort it out."

Darker clouds were approaching, and a curtain of rain blurred the landscape beneath.

"We need to go down. Kalamata is in Greece and the nearest place to take a boat to the yacht. I stay at a small hotel by the ocean and it is pleasantly warm at this time of year. Whatever the outcome at the Tribunal, come away for three days and have a rest."

Patricia sat up and straightened her jacket. "It sounds lovely, but given the complications, I don't think I could... may I think about it?"

"Of course." Anthony's lips brushed her ear and his brown eyes teased her. "Since you are already 'a disgrace' to St. Peter's—you can do anything you want!"

Chapter 19

Patricia woke at 6:20 a.m. with the vibration of her phone under the pillow. It was Clair.

"I'm on my way."

A burst of sobbing shook Clair's shoulders as she opened the front door. "He smiled when I kissed him goodnight. I didn't think he was near the end. David took him a cup of tea at 5:00 a.m. when we got up, but he was gone."

Patricia put her arms around her. Overcome with crying, Clair could say no more.

In Ted's room, David had laid the hospital bed flat. Ted's body lay small and straight like a child's under May's patchwork quilt. His arms rested on top and his eyes were closed. David had rolled a small white towel under Ted's jaw. As a veteran, he had dealt with human death. Patricia was glad it was him, not Clair, who found Ted.

Patricia helped Clair to sit down by the bed and she stroked the brown-and-white spaniel who nestled close. "Oh, Jossie. What are we going to do without him?"

David came in with tea things on a tray. "Hello, Patricia, thanks for coming so quickly."

He put the tray down and took Clair in his arms. "The students are arriving, but Robert is managing everything today."

Patricia walked to look at the garden as David comforted his wife. Anthony and he were brothers, so different in many ways, but alike in sensitivity and kindness.

David kissed Clair's forehead. "The funeral director is on his way. I will walk Jossie to meet him in the lane. I'll be back soon, and Patricia is here with you."

Patricia poured tea, feeling grateful Anthony had Sophie so she could help. She sat Clair down again and put a mug into her hands. "Could you try to drink a little? You are in shock and it will help."

Clair sipped obediently; her gaze locked onto her grandfather. "I told him I would be with him, but I wasn't. I wasn't there to say goodbye."

She sat on the edge of the chair and gripped the mug with both hands. Tears welled again, and Patricia's face was sad.

"I think that Ted wanted to slip away quietly and not grieve you anymore. Jossie was with him, and you gave him the greatest gift. Ted was born in this cottage and you helped him to go from here. It was what he wanted. He knew how much he loved him."

Clair nodded, still watching Ted's face, changing as his body settled. There was no hurry and it was important to take time now. Patricia sat back and picked up her mug of tea. With her parents and Ron, she learned that you cannot grieve until you know for certain the loved one is gone. "Do you remember last Christmas, when Ted was the Innkeeper in your Nativity Ride?"

The corners of Clair's mouth flickered upward. "He was perfect."

"He was. He loved being the patriarch of the Stables, telling the Christmas story with your students and ponies. In the days of the Bible, there was a special way to say goodbye. They do not do it much today, but we could do it for Ted. We could wash his face and hands, and tidy his hair, before he goes with the funeral director."

Clair put down her mug. "Yes, I would like to do that. The caregiver gave him a bed bath last night, and he is wearing his favorite pair of pajamas already."

Patricia fetched a washbowl half-filled with warm water. In the bathroom were two new washcloths, the soap Ted liked, and hand towels. She dipped a washcloth in the warm water, wrung it out and passed it to Clair.

Smoothing her grandfather's face, tears fell again, and she tried to wipe them away.

"Don't hold them back," Patricia whispered. She sat on the other side of the bed, carefully washing and drying Ted's hand. "We weep for love, like Mary, the mother of Jesus and Mary Magdalene, when they washed His body. It is an act of respect and remembrance."

She passed Clair a silver-backed hairbrush. "Ted told me he wished it could have been different, that you had not lost your family. And they lost their son as well, your dad. But he told me you became the daughter he and May never had. He loved you more than words could ever say."

Clair sobbed as she gently brushed Ted's white hair. "He brushed my hair when I was a little girl, but I have never brushed his."

She bent to kiss his cheek and her voice was a child's. "Oh, Granddad, I love you so much."

The tears fell again. "Is he with Grandma May?"

"I am certain that he is."

Patricia carried the washbowl back to the bathroom and found her prayer book. "Tim will come and see you later, but would you like to say a prayer before David and the funeral director come?"

Clair looked at the body in the bed, changing like a fallen leaf in the woods. She was still in shock. "You choose one and I'll listen."

Patricia sat down beside her and took her hand. "Ted liked this one, by Cardinal Newman.

Dear Lord,
We pray that you support us all day long,
Till the shades lengthen and the evening come.
When the busy world is hushed,
Life's fever over, and our work is done,
Then Lord, in your mercy,
Give us safe lodging, and a holy rest at last.
Amen."

David came in with the funeral director and it was tough for Clair. But Patricia knew she had more acceptance that Ted was really gone. The last goodbye would come with the funeral. David was with Clair now, and Patricia went home.

The same infernal racket greeted her from the cottage next door. But when she opened her own front door, Anthony and the dogs gave her a royal welcome. Patricia dropped her bag and walked straight into Anthony's open arms. She rested against his chest, held in such a wonderful man-hug that she wept. Anthony kissed her hair. Patricia felt the steady beat of his heart under her cheek and gave thanks.

* * *

The next day, Patricia was back at Stables Cottage and watched Clair pace the kitchen floor. "I can't bear it. How soon can we hold the funeral and get it over with? I can't cope with people coming back here afterwards. I can't cope with anything right now."

"You are not to worry about this. It is your time to say goodbye to your grandfather and there are no rules. St. Peter's has no booking at all, and I can check Tim's calendar online. Choose a day that is best for you, and we will go from there."

Clair went to the Office to consult with David, Robert,

and Audrey. Patricia pondered the problem. Ted Williams knew so many people, and they were calling to ask when they could pay their respects. How could she organize a memorial event that did not traumatize Clair?

When she came back with the date, Patricia booked Tim's calendar. "How about a winter picnic, the day before Ted's funeral?"

Three days later, everyone who loved Ted Williams, from the Stables, Summerfield village, and farther away met in Potlatch Wood for a celebration.

Robert took the tractor and trailer to St. Mary's and loaded trestle tables and benches. David organized a group of people to pick greenery and decorate the church for the funeral. The Security company guarded the cottage and Patricia went to the Manor House to make soup with Sarah.

They made lots of different kinds and decanted them into borrowed thermos flasks. Sophie stayed safe with Hannibal while they drove to the biggest clearing in Potlatch Wood. Anthony was already there with David as Patricia pulled the little trolley with Sarah. Everything was in it, and they set thermos flasks at regular intervals along the tables. "These are good to hold the Christmas tablecloths down!"

Sarah put out tubs of potato salad, coleslaw, and relish for the hot dogs. "Are you okay for tomorrow? Is it challenging to have the funeral at 10:00 a.m. and a Tenancy Tribunal in Oxford at 2:00 p.m.?"

Patricia shrugged. "It was the only date that worked for the Stables and Tim Fell, so I just booked it in."

Clair and David were supplying the hot dogs and sodas. Clair wore a Christmas apron over her jeans as she turned wieners on the barbecue. She called out, "This was an inspired idea! It's a lot easier to talk if my hands are busy."

People arrived, warmly wrapped, calling greetings as they piled homemade bread, muffins, and desserts onto the tables. Anthony supervised kids with building a bonfire away from the trees. He grinned at Patricia, who gave her thumbs up sign, and she grinned back. It was chilly, but pale winter sun broke through the mist. Kids raced around the clearing as Anthony lit the bonfire, and there was cheering as the flames spiraled upward. He had a rake to poke the branches and David joined him with another. Patricia smiled, remembering Ron with Paul, and how much boys love playing with bonfires!

The sausages were ready and keeping warm in foil containers when Clair's students in wheelchairs arrived with their families. Sarah joined Patricia to help serve, and everyone was pouring sodas.

Vulnerable youngsters can only stay a short while in the cold, so David called everyone together. He held Clair's hand to climb onto a bench, so that everyone could hear. She looked around at all the faces and almost lost it. She gulped, "Granddad would tell me to get on with it, so we can eat."

Everyone laughed. That was exactly what Ted would say!

"Thank you all for coming. Granddad considered himself lucky to spend his entire life in Summerfield, working with animals and sharing this country life with people like you."

A faint gleam of winter sun lit Clair's face and she raised her cup of soda. "May I ask you to toast him with me? For a life well lived and everything he gave us—to Ted!"

Everyone lifted their cups, "To Ted!"

It was a splendid picnic. Patricia and Sarah served all the hot dogs and took their own to sit at a table opposite Anthony and Robert. Patricia spotted Jim earlier and avoided eye contact. But Audrey sat down next to her, with Jim on her other side and they appeared to be HOLDING HANDS!

Patricia looked the other way and passed the tomato ketchup to Sarah, "Is it on the grapevine that I'm in a Tenancy Tribunal tomorrow?"

Mouth full of hot dog, Sarah nodded and Patricia took a squishy bite. Anthony laughed, "You could play Dracula, with all that ketchup on your face!"

She wrinkled her nose at him and wiped her face with a napkin. Sarah finished the hot dog and sighed. "Enough of sophisticated recipes, nothing beats a hot dog in the open air."

Patricia added, "With friends."

Through the sweet-smelling smoke from the bonfire, she saw Clair laughing, with folks telling funny stories about Ted. David was on bonfire duty, supervising the kids toasting marshmallows on long sticks.

When the students in wheelchairs waved to everybody and departed, it was time to pack up before it got dark. Sarah loaded the trolley with Patricia. "I hope you get a decent judge tomorrow. What happens if they don't get evicted?"

Patricia blew out her breath. "They will feel free to do anything they want, and I cannot get another Tribunal date for six months."

They pulled the trolley back to the car and Sarah changed hands. "Anthony mentioned in confidence that he invited you to Kalamata. I can have Sophie with Hannibal if you want to go."

"You are a dear friend and I would love a brief vacation. But do you think I should go?"

Sarah's brow wrinkled as they packed everything into Patricia's car. "You guys are getting on so well, but Anthony is more serious than you about a relationship."

Patricia stopped and looked at her. "Surely he's not looking for marriage?"

Clair arrived at that moment and gave them both a hug. "Thank you for making this happen. Granddad would have loved his memorial and I can cope with tomorrow."

Chapter 20

The next day, Patricia stood in the porch of St. Peter's wearing her verger's robe. It was 9:49 a.m., and all was in place for Ted's funeral.

A single bell tolled. Anthony wore a dark suit, collared shirt, and tie, and stood with the bell ringer from St. Mary's. Tim Fell went forward to meet Clair and David, and both hugged Patricia as they entered the porch. Distant applause alerted them to the funeral cortege approaching. People lined the sidewalks along the only Summerfield street to bid farewell to a man who was a local legend. Ted Williams, last coachman to the Old Duke, rode to his funeral in a magnificent Victorian hearse, drawn by his own black horses.

Robert brought Blackbird and Rebel to a halt at the front gate of the church. Their coats shone like polished ebony and long manes rippled down from tall, black plumes on their heads. Ted's coffin, surrounded by floral tributes, was visible inside the glass-sided coach.

The funeral director walked forward to open the rear door. He wore a black tailcoat, breeches, black shoes, and a black top hat.

"Whoa, stand up."

At Robert's command, the horses were still. Seated on

the driver's box, he wore an identical outfit to the funeral director. The scene reminded Patricia of a Victorian etching she had seen in the Oxford museum.

Jim and three ushers, all wearing modern black suits, stepped forward to slide the coffin onto the wheeled bier. Top hat off, the funeral director led up the path to bring the coffin into St. Peter's. Patricia quietly raised a hand and the bell ceased tolling. St. Mary's choir sang *Abide with Me* as Ted's coffin progressed up the central aisle to the altar rail. Tim Fell followed with Clair and David. Patricia glanced back as Robert spoke quietly to his horses. The black hearse pulled slowly away.

Inside the church, Anthony had roped off the area by the organ and laid dustsheets. People filled every available seat. Holly and ivy cascaded from window ledges. Clair and David had brought a gigantic Christmas tree and strung it with shimmering lights for Ted. On a table next to it stood two large photographs in silver frames. One was a picture of Ted, wearing the Duke's livery and driving the open carriage at Royal Ascot. The other was Clair's favorite, her grandparents on their wedding day at St. Peter's.

Tim led the welcoming prayers, and the congregation sang *All Things Bright and Beautiful*. During the hymn, Anthony moved quietly to stand next to Patricia. Hidden by the folds of her robe, she took his hand and squeezed it gently. Anthony returned the pressure before they dropped hands to stand on duty again.

Tim conducted the Church of England funeral service from the Book of Common Prayer. "Earth to earth, ashes to ashes, dust to dust."

Ted had requested no eulogy, and everyone stood in silence as the choir sang *Joy to the World*. The ushers wheeled the bier with his coffin out of the church. Tim followed with Clair and David, to witness burial in the Williams family plot.

When they left, Patricia and Anthony moved into the shadows by the back room. Today, they were the silent servants of St. Peter's, watching as people talked quietly and gathered their things. It was a sad occasion, but Patricia felt satisfaction that the church was alive today. Ted was baptized at St. Peter's, married here, and in death, received for burial.

The funeral director returned to check with Patricia that everything was complete, and they shook hands. From the corner of her eye, she saw Tim Fell escort Clair and David to a waiting limo before he joined them.

"Thanks to you all. Clair said it was exactly as Ted had wanted it and Jim is filling the grave now."

Anthony turned off lights and Patricia collected the extra Order of Service booklets. Tim went into the robing room and reappeared in civilian clothes, wheeling his bike. "See you on Sunday."

He walked down the path with the funeral director. Patricia smiled at Anthony as she put on her coat. "It is all in a day's work for them, but I am glad we don't do this too often. Is there time to visit Ted?"

Anthony nodded and held up his keys. "I will finish locking up."

Patricia sat on Ted's bench, looking at the earth mounded over the grave and the floral tributes laid on top. Mist still hung over the yew trees as Anthony joined her. "Clair ordered a new headstone, and I love her beautiful sheaf of lilies."

Clair's flowers lay next to the tribute from the Duke, grandson of the one Ted had worked for. The wreath was the size of a cartwheel, decorated in horse-racing colors. Patricia thought it was a bit overboard, but bent to read the card, which was embossed with a gold Coat of Arms.

For Ted Williams,
    Grateful thanks for dedicated service over so many years.
    Hugh

Patricia sat back on the bench. "I'm glad that Clair did so well."

Anthony took her hand. "She did. Are you okay for this afternoon?"

Patricia smiled at him. "You are always so supportive! I'm tired but have prayed for Heavenly help. Your idea of printing copies for the Adjudicator was a good one."

Anthony grinned, "The fish and chips were good too!"

Summerfield's fish-and-chip van had provided dinner last night. They sat on the couch in front of the fire, with the dogs. Wearing headphones, they went through her presentation one last time. Nothing was said but Patricia felt sad that Anthony and Hannibal would soon go home.

Pulling her thoughts back to the present, Patricia focused on Ted. He had been a larger-than-life character with a heart of gold, and his passing marked the end of an era. Patricia stood up, "Goodbye, old friend. I will miss seeing you."

Anthony stood beside her. "Rest in peace, Ted."

* * *

The Security guard spoke to them through the window of his van. "The two women left in the black car with the baby about twenty minutes ago."

There was no sign of the motorcycle and Patricia greeted the dogs, so happy to see them. She was about to let them out into the backyard but stopped. Through the glass she saw that from next door, they had thrown large trash bags over the fence. The plastic had split, and the disgusting contents blew everywhere. Broken glass glinted on the path.

Seeing her face, Anthony came over. "Donna is aiming to make you emotional in the Tribunal."

Patricia turned from the door and ran her hands through her hair. "I am angry, not tearful. She cares nothing for anyone, and the broken glass was for the dogs. Could we take them to Sarah now, pick up your car, and grab a sandwich from the deli? I want to be at the Tribunal before Donna arrives."

Anthony nodded and pulled out his phone. "She may think the mess will make us late. Security has a Haz-Mat clean-up team who can come in through the back gate. Donna is betting everything to stop you."

Patricia was hurrying up the stairs to change. She called back. "She will lose that bet."

* * *

The Oxford Tenancy Tribunal met every weekday in Room 325 of the Court House. Landlords came to protest about tenants and vice versa. Each presented their own case and could bring one supporter. The Adjudicator was a local judge. The decision was legal and binding on all parties.

Seated in the Waiting Room, Patricia could not help but laugh when Donna and Tracey walked in. They were dressed in the same clothes as when she first showed them the cottage. Donna also wore glasses with her hair scraped back into the same tight bun. Patricia shook her head at her own gullibility. She had learned a hard lesson being what Sarah called *a bit of a do-gooder.* Tracey pushed the stroller with the baby, who had red cheeks, as if he were teething. Both women glared at Patricia.

At 2:00 p.m., a woman wearing a *Registrar* badge called

them into Room 325. A raised dais stood between two desks and Patricia walked to the one marked, *Landlord*. She gave three sets of photocopies to the Recorder. "One is for the Adjudicator; one, for Mrs. Smithers, and the third is for your records."

"Thank you. All rise for Justice Melrose."

The Adjudicator entered and seated herself at the desk on the dais. She was a professional woman in her forties, with brown hair, wearing a dark suit. She scanned the photocopied documents. Unseen, Anthony placed his hand between Patricia's shoulder blades for a few moments, and she felt his comforting presence.

A light glowed on the console and the Recorder adjusted her microphone. "Testing, testing. This is Case 5, *Anderson versus Smithers, Tenancy Abuse,* recorded for documentation and appeal. Mrs. Anderson, please state your case."

Patricia felt confident as she rose to speak. She wore a royal blue pant suit from her working days, with a white shirt under the jacket. "Your Honor, I own a joined property, Halfmoon Cottages, in the village of Summerfield. I live at Number 1 and rented Number 2 to Mrs. Smithers. Page one of my document has a picture of the cottages, so you can see how people can impact the lives of those living next door. The reverse has a photocopy of the Tenancy Agreement, signed by Mrs. Smithers and me."

Patricia waited until the Adjudicator finished reading and looked at her again. "I wish to present evidence that Mrs. Smithers has irretrievably broken the Tenancy Agreement and ask for an Eviction Order."

Tracey's baby had been whimpering and she repeatedly pushed a pacifier into its mouth. Now she stopped and there was a yell of outrage from the infant. The Recorder paused the recording, "Mrs. Smithers, please ask your supporter to wait outside."

Donna turned to Tracey who immediately lifted her top, undid the nursing bra, and plugged the baby onto her breast.

Patricia blinked. The lawyer had warned her of women who used children to avoid eviction. Donna's voice was pitiful. "Your Honor, I need my daughter here. That woman scares us. We are trying to live quiet lives and bring up a baby, but she wants to throw us out, when we have nowhere to go."

Thinking of Donna's behavior, and the filth in her back-yard, Patricia was furious. But she kept her face neutral as the Recorder indicated she should continue. "Page Two of my evidence is a police report from a raid on Number 2, Halfmoon Cottages. The police found drugs and stolen property. By allowing the use of illegal drugs and storing stolen items, Mrs. Smithers broke the Tenancy Agreement."

Donna jumped to her feet. "That's not my fault!"

The Recorder motioned her to sit down. "Please do not interrupt. You will have your turn after Mrs. Anderson."

Patricia calmly turned the page. "Page Three lists the antisocial behavior, with dates, when the tenant, her family and others caused considerable nuisance at the property. The reverse has dated photographs of their parking abuses, littering, and damage."

Donna stared at Patricia. She had not opened her photocopies, and Patricia continued. "The next page has transcripts of verbal abuse and personal threats by Mrs. Smithers against me, her Landlord. I am passing original recordings, verified by Ecclesiastical Security Company, to the Recorder. Last, I submit copies of the three Written Warnings served on Mrs. Smithers by an Oxford legal firm. Each is a request that she cease breaking the Tenancy Agreement, or risk eviction."

Patricia's heart pounded. She looked up at the Adjudicator. "Mrs. Smithers has chosen to stop paying rent and ignored the Written Warnings. I request an Eviction Order, to remove her from the tenancy and my property."

Patricia sat down. There was a pause while the Recorder sorted her notes and then she looked at Donna. "Mrs. Smithers, you may speak now."

Donna twisted her hands together. "That woman is a nosy, interfering landlord, who fusses over every little noise and our music at family gatherings. She trespassed on our property, forcing me to stop paying the rent. We have a baby, but she does not control her vicious dogs."

She switched to pleading. "It is Christmas. You would not evict a defenseless child at Christmas. Give me another chance and I will pay the arrears in instalments."

The Adjudicator leaned forward, "Do you have any evidence to oppose Mrs. Anderson's request for an Eviction Order?"

Donna's face was blotchy with anger. "I don't have time for that sort of rubbish! Only old busybodies like her do this. She looks down on us and … "

Justice Melrose banged her gavel. "Thank you. I have considered the evidence presented in this case and find in favor of the Landlord. The Eviction Order is granted."

She left the way she had entered, and Donna stormed out. Tracey followed with the baby and Patricia went forward to receive the Eviction Order. "Thank you."

The Recorder glanced around and lowered her voice. "The recording machine is off. Confidentially, I want to thank you too. That woman has been in front of us four times in as many years. She reckons on getting a different Adjudicator each time, but I have heard the same story over and over. She targets new landlords, who do not understand the evidence needed for an Eviction Order. At last, Donna Smithers got what she deserved. Happy Holidays!"

Outside, Patricia told Anthony what she said, and he grinned. "Well done! Tea at your favorite teashop before we go back? It will be a pleasure to have the Security team escort those people off your property."

While they waited for tea, Anthony called Security. "Really? We will be back in an hour."

He clicked off his phone. "A white van has arrived with a trailer and they are moving out. I talked with the Security team earlier and asked them to have five guys there today. Donna and Co. will not trash the place before they leave, unlike the tenants at my London apartment."

Patricia sighed; all her energy spent. "I could never have done this without you. I cannot thank you enough."

"I helped, but you presented the data professionally to win." Anthony selected a scone with cream and jam from the cake stand. "I need to go to Kalamata tomorrow. I bought you a ticket just in case. Why don't you pack a few things, stay at the Manor House tonight and fly with me tomorrow?"

Patricia sipped her tea and hesitated, "I'm anxious about leaving the cottages."

Anthony cut his scone down the middle, spread the cream, and took a bite. "Um… not as good as Sarah's."

He chewed. "You could book a 24-hour security watch. They would also check for booby traps and change the locks. The hazard crew can deep clean and you can look at it all again when we get back."

"Okay, those are good ideas. Thank you, I'd love a few days in Greece. But could someone else drive us to the airport? I can't face small talk with Jim all the way to Heathrow!"

Chapter 21

The owner of the small Kalamata hotel came smiling to greet them and Anthony introduced Patricia. She was amazed to hear him conversing in fluent Greek as they walked into Reception. Beyond the white deck, the Mediterranean Sea gleamed a sparkling azure as the sun set. Patricia breathed deeply. Herbs and sea salt scented the air and transported her to another world.

The hotel was modern and built on three levels in traditional Greek style. It had white walls, a terracotta roof, and balconies with scarlet geraniums tumbling from hanging baskets.

Anthony handed her a key, and they walked across a courtyard to some stairs. "We have the best rooms in the hotel, on the top floor overlooking the beach. I am next door to you, and we have time for a quick shower before dinner."

Patricia opened the door to her room and pulled back the white, net drapes. Sliding the door, she stepped onto the balcony and gazed at tiny white waves whispering along the shoreline. Palm fronds rustled in the gentle breeze as lamps came on in the gardens and reflected in the turquoise swimming pool. They had furnished her bathroom and double bedroom in Greek prints and fabrics. It was all immaculately clean and Patricia lay down on the bed for a few minutes with her head on a crisp, white pillow. She sighed with relief that Anthony had persuaded her to come. Then she made herself get up and shower before she fell asleep!

They met again at the foot of the stairs. Anthony wore a pale-blue polo shirt with chinos and Patricia had chosen a pink floral top with long sleeves, to go with her soft fawn slacks. They walked across the courtyard to the restaurant and he took her hand. "You look lovely, and a glass of excellent Greek wine will complete the picture."

"Thank you, I am ready for that. You have trimmed your beard. Have you ever been clean-shaven?"

Anthony ran a hand over his white beard. "Not for a long time, it's a part of who I am now."

A smiling young waiter seated them at a table by the window. After a moment, Patricia whispered. "Anthony, I don't know what to order. The menu is in Greek."

Quietly, Anthony turned it over, revealing English on the other side. She grinned at him. "Duh, as my grand-daughters would say!"

He poured her a glass of wine while she went back and forth between the Greek and English versions. He poured sparkling water with slices of lemon and then pointed to an item on the menu. "Do you like seafood? They have succulent giant prawns as a starter."

Patricia put aside the menu and picked up her glass. "I will have whatever you choose tonight and start my Greek lessons tomorrow."

Anthony raised his glass. "Here's to a relaxing break."

She smiled and clinked glasses, "I will drink to that. Cheers!"

Two smiling young men set out their meal. A basket of fresh bread, brown and crumbly with big seeds, was accompanied by Greek salads in beautiful pottery bowls. There were slices of ripe tomato, green pepper, and cucumber, with Kalamata olives. Then came the sizzling seafood platter. Patricia took a deep breath. "Bliss!"

The main dish was souvlakia; tender pieces of lamb, grilled on skewers at the table, served with rice and vegetables. Savoring each fresh taste, chatting with Anthony about everything except the recent horror at home, Patricia felt her spirits lift. Was it the wine? The delicious food, or the company? Perhaps it was a combination of them all and she was a little tipsy. Suddenly, fatigue overwhelmed her and Patricia passed her hand across her eyes.

Anthony stood up and reached for her hand. "Come along, you need sleep."

Climbing the stairs, she let him lead and pull her gently behind him. He unlocked the door for her. "When you wake tomorrow, I will be on my way to the yacht and back twenty-four hours after that, by about 8:00 a.m., so I will see you at breakfast then. I have booked a rental car for the day and we can go adventuring."

Anthony gave her a gentle hug and a kiss on the cheek. "Sleep well, I'm just next door if you need me."

Patricia prepared for bed, and a text came through from Sarah.

Hi! No sign of rats at the cottage. We are having fun and hope that you are too.
    Love, Sarah, Sophie, and Hannibal xxx

It was 11:00 p.m. and chilly. Patricia snuggled beneath clean white sheets and a soft velour blanket.

Dear Lord, please keep them all safe at home. Thank you for the gift of this beautiful place and thank you for Anthony.

Waking at 7:30 a.m., Patricia leaned up on one elbow. Dazzling sunshine touched everything. Wearing a light hotel robe over her pajamas, she ate breakfast sitting at the table on her balcony. There was not a single cloud in the blue sky and the ocean sparkled. A mountain across the bay looked smokey blue, and sparrows chirped in the pink bougainvillea.

Patricia thought she should go out and explore, but her exhausted body thought otherwise. It felt like she was convalescing after some awful sickness. She hung the Do Not Disturb sign on the door, drew the thick drapes, and went back to sleep.

During the day, Patricia drank lots of cool, bottled water from the fridge and slept on and off with no motivation to go anywhere. Sunset touched everything with pink, peach, and orange. The ocean turned silver; the hump of the mountain silhouetted against the sky. Patricia ordered dinner and a small carafe of wine in her room. She acknowledged Sarah's text that all was well and resisted turning on the TV. Patricia was in bed early and woke at 7:00 a.m. the next morning feeling like a new woman!

She crossed the courtyard to where Anthony sat reading a newspaper in the shade. He wore formal black pants with a white shirt, and black Oxford shoes. His tie, jacket, and briefcase lay on another chair. He bent his head, studying an article in the paper, and she thought what an attractive man he was.

"Good morning! Did you have a pleasant trip?"

Anthony stood up to hold a chair out for her. "Lovely to see you. Sadly, it was not a pleasant trip; but coffee and a big breakfast are on their way."

Patricia indicated his outfit and smiled. "Not taking this vacation thing too seriously, are we?"

She was wearing relaxed denim jeans and a white applique T-shirt. Bare feet were in white sandals and she had painted her toenails geranium red. The waiter arrived with muesli, Greek yogurt and honey, scrambled eggs, toast, and coffee and spread it on their table.

"I'll change after breakfast. I need to dress formally for Dad, or he doesn't take things seriously."

"How did the meeting go?"

Anthony drizzled honey onto Greek yogurt. "Do you remember when Hannibal hit Ted's chicken run?"

Patricia laughed, remembering squawking, barking, and general pandemonium. Anthony smiled too. "It was like that. The Captain was pleased to see me, but Dad was furious, and I upset the caregiver. There are sixty years between them, but he says he is in love. I saw the young woman privately and explained that he had no money. It is all tied up in the business and specifically excludes anyone who marries him. She would get nothing when he died."

Anthony poured coffee for them both. "I felt sorry for her and gave her a big bonus. She left without saying goodbye to Dad and he blamed me. He is sulking. I need to find another care agency. The Captain requested a male caregiver, preferably Greek!"

* * *

After breakfast, Anthony changed his clothes and drove Patricia along the coast of the Gulf of Messina. "This peninsular has a backbone of mountains and fertile soil. It is strategically important on the Mediterranean. The Greeks, Romans, Turks, and British fought over it for centuries."

Driving on the right side of the road did not feel at all 'right' to Patricia! She closed her eyes as they drove over the mountain and was happier when they reached the villages. Anthony found a thousand-year-old church, with wonderful frescos and Patricia loved the craft stalls. Lunch was in the village of Kardamili, with a lizard who sat motionless in an olive tree beside them. "He's like a tiny prehistoric monster."

Anthony leaned back, comfortable in his chinos and a dark-green T-shirt. "There's a legend about old olives trees. Zeus, the Father of the Greek Gods, admired an old couple who lived together faithfully all their lives and offered them one wish. They asked to be together for all eternity so he turned them into an olive tree." He pointed at an old olive tree, "If you look, you can see their arms, tightly wrapped around each other."

On their way back to Kalamata, Anthony drove inland to the Greek ruins at Ancient Messini. "I want to show you a spectacular temple and amphitheater, right at the top of a mountain pass."

The path from the car to the ruins wandered through tall grasses with blond seed heads. Huge white clouds floated in the blue sky above them and cast cloud-shaped shadows over the landscape as they floated past. Anthony pointed, "See the tall, dark, cypress trees, standing between the olives? The Greeks fought a significant battle there. Cyprus trees are like our yew trees at home; they mark a burial ground."

Patricia perched on the edge of a step with the stone pillars behind her. In the far distance, the Mediterranean shone soft lavender, and the coastline was like the cut edge of a jigsaw puzzle. Anthony came to sit next to her. "I want a selfie together here."

She posed, leaning against him, smiling, and he took the photograph with his phone. Then he held her hand. "This is one of my favorite places in Greece. I brought you here to ask if you would marry me?"

He was looking down at their clasped hands. He did not see the look on Patricia's face. Sarah was right again! Anthony looked up again. "I've reached my sixties. At last I have found a woman I love and admire so much, I cannot live without her. I thought it was not worth asking, as I cannot offer you a long life. But I talked with David before we came away."

"What did he say?"

"That last year, I told him he had one chance to ask Clair. She might say no, but if he did not ask, she could not say yes. He said we only have one life and I should take the same chance with you. Would you marry me, Patricia?"

Patricia bit her lip. Why could she not immediately say yes and reassure him of a happily ever after? But something inside held her back. "I didn't understand that you were thinking of marriage, when I was thinking of a close friendship."

"It's the Parkinson's, isn't it?" Anthony hurried on. "I am fighting it and there are excellent medications. I can pay for nursing care, and there could be a cure. I don't want to be alone anymore, and I have fallen in love with you, Patricia. I long to hold you in my arms while I still can."

Patricia squeezed his hand. "Oh, Anthony, you are the dearest of friends; but since Ron died, I have not wanted to date, let alone marry again."

She blushed and looked down. "I am also not interested in the physical side of marriage. My hormones have gone. I feel past all that."

Anthony threw back his head and roared with laughter. "Oh no! I find the woman of my dreams, but she does not want me physically. Dearest Patricia, you are very desirable, and my spirit would be more than willing but don't be alarmed, the flesh has grown decidedly weak! But I know you like to cuddle."

Patricia thought of hugs at the cottage and sweet kisses at the top of the tower. She smiled. "You are right. I have enjoyed cuddling with you. But I sleep diagonally across my double bed, with Sophie on the floor beside me—and I cannot sleep with someone snoring."

Anthony's eyes danced. "I am with you there and relegated Hannibal to the landing outside my bedroom. But we have four beautiful suites at the Manor House, all with their own bathroom. My parents slept in separate rooms, as do our Queen and the Duke of Edinburgh. Could we do the same?"

Anxiety clouded Patricia's face. "I owe you so much, I…"

Anthony held up a hand. "Stop right there! This has nothing to do with owing anybody anything. Hannibal and I came to Summerfield as failures. With you, we feel needed and wanted. You saved our lives. I love you, and I want to marry you for sharing and fun, to do things together, laugh, and relax."

She shook her head as if trying to clear it. "I have made quick decisions and lived to regret them. Could we enjoy the rest of the trip and talk some more at home?"

Anthony tried to be lighthearted. "Okay, let's walk some more. I guess it's better than a straight no, but only if you understand that all I want for Christmas is you."

Chapter 22

In the Arrivals area at Heathrow, Anthony sat in the front seat with Sarah and Patricia slid into the back seat of the 4 x 4 to hug an excited Sophie! Feathery tail waving, she tried to cover Patricia's face in big wet licks.

"Whoa, Sophie! How is my lovely girl? Hi Sarah! Thank you so much for having her and coming to get us. She's looking great!"

Sarah started the engine and pulled out into the flow of traffic. Outside the airport it was a late afternoon, grey and raining, and Patricia was glad for her coat again. Goodbye, sunny Kalamata; they were back to England in December!

"I did not bring Hannibal in case we got stuck somewhere. You both look wonderful. Was it warm?"

"Fabulous!" Patricia raved about the Mediterranean, the lovely hotel, and delicious food. She was relieved when Anthony took over, telling Sarah about his father and making her laugh. Patricia cuddled Sophie and listened as they headed back to Summerfield. Sarah made eye contact with her in the rearview mirror. "They completed the repairs on Number 2 and all the cleaning. Robert said Donna and Co. are in London, so the Security firm has finished now."

Patricia leaned forward, "What a relief!"

Anthony turned to smile, "Hopefully, the nightmare is behind you."

Sarah nodded. "Hannibal will miss Sophie when she goes home. They are almost inseparable, but she's definitely the boss now!"

They reached Summerfield at 7:00 p.m. It was raining and cold. Halfmoon Cottages were both in darkness. There were no sports shoes over the power lines, and no tenant vehicles. Anthony carried Patricia's bag to the door, and she hugged her purse to her chest. She wanted to cry out, "Please, don't go!"

What came out was, "Thank you so much for taking me to Kalamata. It was amazing."

Anthony hesitated. "Would you like to meet tomorrow?"

Patricia nodded, "I'll call you."

She waved as they drove away. Both yards were clear of trash, but it was spookily quiet. She opened the back door for Sophie to race down the garden path. They had changed the locks on Number 2 and a set of new keys lay on the kitchen counter. Patricia fed Sophie and made a quick dinner of eggs with toast. She ate it on a tray, catching up on TV news. She did not mean to fall asleep; but woke two hours later with a crick in her neck. She missed Anthony.

There was a Welcome Home text from Clair, but the battery on her mobile phone was low, so she sent a quick reply.

All good here and glad with you too. Battery low, Will call for big catch up tomorrow.
Love to both. xxx.

Sophie sat looking expectantly at her leash.

"You had a long day in the car, so we will do a quick walk around St. Peter's."

Patricia plugged in her mobile phone to charge on

the countertop and clipped Sophie's leash to her harness. Slipping on her red quilted coat, she switched off the kitchen lights. Then she turned them back on again. "It will be more welcoming when we come back."

The rain had stopped, but the wind had risen and growled through the trees. The bright moon, three-quarters full, could be seen between the swiftly moving clouds. Patricia locked the door and put her keys into the strappy purse carried diagonally across her body. She could only find one glove, so stuck one hand in her pocket and held Sophie's leash with the other. "Come on, let's walk and be back soon!"

Sophie surged ahead on the extending leash, sniffing, and exploring. Patricia looked back at her cottage and it glowed. The other side was dark, and the warmth of Kalamata was already a memory.

"We must go into Number 2 tomorrow," she informed Sophie. "I need to go to the rental agency in Banbury. And what on earth am I going to do about Anthony?"

Walking under the streetlamps to the back gate of the church, Patricia thought about marriage. She came to Summerfield to be independent. Would it be the end of her project at St. Peter's? Anthony's wife would have certain duties, let alone dealing with advancing Parkinson's disease. Five years on, she was through grieving for Ron. Could she do it all again? Anthony was her dear friend, but would marriage complicate it?

Patricia looked up at the church as they walked, her feelings for Anthony wafting this way and that in the wind. Suddenly, Sophie halted, ears up and nose pointing into the darkness. Patricia's heartbeat pounded. Was there a faint light shining up from the crypt? Was Anthony here?

She stood at the top of the steep steps. The door at the bottom was ajar and a thin beam of light shone out. Sophie pulled back, like last time, and Patricia put the reel down next to her. "Stay, then. I won't be a moment."

Holding onto the handrail, she went cautiously down. "Anthony? Are you here?"

Pushing open the door, she took two steps inside. She saw a box from the Food Bank and a sleeping bag. The inner sliding door was half open, and light shone from the interior. "Anthony?"

Somebody jumped from behind the door and shoved her in the middle of her back. Cannoning into the wall, Patricia grabbed hold to save herself and fell to her knees on the sleeping bag. A dark figure jumped through the gap and out of the door, slamming it shut.

The key turned in the lock and Patricia struggled to her feet, "No!"

Feet ran up the steps and she beat on the door. "Come back! Please come back! Don't leave me here!"

She listened for returning feet, then thought of Sophie. If he, and Patricia was sure it was a man, tried to grab her, Sophie would run. Frantically, Patricia fumbled in her purse for her mobile phone. Would it work down here? But no familiar shape fitted into her hand and with horror, she remembered where it was!

Then the lights went out.

In the darkness, Patricia turned and felt her way to sit down with her back against the door. Anthony had switched the lights on from the external electricity box. They were on a timer. Whoever was here had kept the door open to turn on the light again when it cut out. But where did he get the keys to the crypt? And where was Sophie?

Patricia fought her panic and prayed, "Please Lord, please look after Sophie."

Anthony thought she would call him tomorrow. But what if she did not call? Would he avoid her, thinking she was saying no to marriage? Even if he came to work at St. Peter's tomorrow, why would he open the crypt? Patricia nibbled her thumbnail, which she had not done since she was a teenager. It was cold, and her knees hurt. She shivered in the pitch-black darkness and a great sob rose in her throat. The man had shut her in and Anthony only came back after a year. She would be dead by then.

Then the vent by the organ came into her mind. If she could climb onto the broad ledge of funerary jars, she could breathe through it. If Anthony or anyone else came into the church, they would hear her shouting. Patricia trembled to think of crossing the crypt in total darkness. Maybe she should wait until morning? Surely there would be more light showing.

She spoke out loud to push back the dark and give herself courage. "Do it quickly, before you totally freak out."

Crawling forward on hands and knees, Patricia felt for the inner steel door and slid it fully open.

She listened intently. With widened eyes and prickly skin, she felt the claustrophobia of the lead-lined vault. But then her heart leaped because in the distance was a faint pattern of light. There were dots in a square where the moonlight shone through the grille over the vent by the organ.

"Dear Lord and all my guardian angels, please help me now."

Holding onto the door, Patricia stood up and took a tentative step. Focusing on the pinpricks of light, she reached in front of her and found the edge of the first table tomb. "Yes!"

Feeling along it, she held onto a marble foot and reached for the next tomb. How had Anthony walked across? She retraced his route in her mind. Left here and then turn right to face the vent. The dots were a tiny lighthouse to guide her.

But there was a whisper of cobwebs and Patricia thrashed with her arms. "Ahhhhhhhh!"

Her shout was too loud for inside the crypt, and startled, she jumped forward, stubbing her toe.

She sobbed, "No spiders, no spiders! Anthony, I'm shut in, please, please, find me!"

Patricia held onto a stone corner as she fought to regain control. "Stop it, stop now! You are a grown woman. You can do this."

Tears in her eyes, she timidly reached out again, and her fingers found the little dog. It was like the one in the church upstairs and she caressed his marble ears, "Oh, Sophie, I wish you were here."

Then Patricia gave a quiet laugh. "But you're such a scaredy-cat, I would have to carry *you*!"

She prayed Sophie would be safe as she felt her way along the side of the knight's tomb. Across the gap to another. Patricia blinked and stared into the dark. Where were the lights? There they were. The moon must have been behind a cloud, and the faint patterns of the vent became her guiding star again.

At last! She stood below the ledge with one hand on the wall and a breath of clean air in her nose. "It is not too high. Get up there and you can rest."

The lead ended in raw stone around the vent. Patricia got a handhold and pulled herself up with one knee onto the ledge.

Then she hit a jar. "Oh, no!"

Two seconds later, it hit the floor in a burst of porcelain and human dust.

Patricia flung herself onto the ledge and thrust her face into her coat sleeve. "Ugh! That is DISGUSTING!"

She breathed slowly, shuddering like Sophie shaking water from her coat. But she had made it! Slowly, Patricia sat up and felt for the other funerary jars. One crash was one too many. She moved them, one by one, to the far end of the ledge so she could lie down with her face by the vent.

With her last strength, Patricia undid the buckle of her purse strap and hooked it through some holes in the vent. Buckled again, the strap tethered her so there was no danger of rolling off the ledge. Pulling up her hood to make a pillow, Patricia breathed gratefully against the holes of the vent and looked through one, like a peephole.

Pale moonlight flooded St. Peter's spilling colors onto the floor through the stained-glass windows. Above the altar, *Jesus, the Light of the World* was there and Michael, her Archangel, in the window. Patricia sobbed. She was not alone but must wait and endure. Florence, Anthony's mother, came into her mind. She had died so young and his father had shut her in the crypt. But Anthony had rescued her, and she was his guardian angel.

You change as soon as you change your mind.

Christmas is coming. A new birth and New Year. A chance to begin again. Patricia relived her walks with Anthony and the dogs. She remembered the carousel, sitting by the fire in her cottage, and the fun of playing Broadway musicals to get even with Donna! Anthony, not she, was getting things moving at St. Peter's. He had gently kissed her at the top of the tower. He had taken her to beautiful Kalamata.

Was it enough for a marriage?

We are only on earth for a short while and love balances equally with the dark. Will you refuse love and light because you are afraid of being hurt? Light and dark are always there in equal measure. But without love, you are already dead, and Anthony is a prince among men.

If I get out of here, I will say yes.

Patricia shouted, "Help! Anthony! Help! Help!"

But there was not enough oxygen and her throat was full of dust. Tears slid from under closed eyelids.

Anthony would not find her in time and she would die in the Bartlett-Brown crypt. "Lord, now lettest thou thy servant depart in peace according to thy word."

* * *

Did she sleep?

The main door slammed back against the wall and Hannibal's joyful barking reached the rafters. The lights went on. Patricia struggled to call, but her voice would not work. Paws skittered across the stone tiles and the wet nose of a tattered guardian angel snuffled against the vent.

She heard Anthony's voice. "What have you got there, Hannibal? Good Lord, she is in the crypt! Hang on, sweetheart, my keys are in the car."

Lights went on in the crypt and Patricia felt the draft suck through the vent.

Anthony's firm hands unbuckled the strap and helped her down, supporting her outside and into the night air. "Hannibal heard Sophie outside. She was by the kitchen door, trailing her leash. We raced to the cottage in the car and your kitchen was a blaze of light, but the door was locked. Your phone was on charge and I was desperate that they had taken you."

Sitting at the top of the steps, wrapped in his arms with Sophie near, Patricia cried.

Anthony gently touched the marks where tears left tracks through the grime. "It's okay, it's okay. You are safe. I've got you now."

Patricia held him tight and croaked, "How did you find me?"

"It was Hannibal. I had one of your sweaters in the car, gave it to him, and told him to seek. He went off like a rocket on the end of his leash with Sophie, along the route you must have taken. We passed the front door of the church and he doubled back, barking like crazy. He went straight to the vent! But how did you get into the crypt? I was so afraid for you—and we need each other. Darling, please marry me."

Patricia leaned into his warmth; her head cradled by his shoulder. She rasped, "Yes, yes, please."

Anthony bent his head, "Did you say yes?"

Patricia raised her head and cleared her throat. She looked up into anxious brown eyes. "Anthony, I love your light and kindness. And I love *you*. Please, let's get married!"

Chapter 23

Two days of recovering and Patricia could not believe how fast things moved! Sarah helped her bring some things from the cottage and move into the guest suite at the Manor House. Patricia knew that she had changed. Home was in the heart. Joy was here, with Anthony, Sophie, and Hannibal.

Patricia shuffled her lace-edged pillows to sit up in bed. She luxuriated in the elegant four-poster bed with its rose tapestry hangings. Outside the long windows of her first-floor bedroom was a chilly December day. Inside, it glowed with pretty table lamps, light oak furniture, and soft rose, deep pile carpet. Sophie had gone to find Hannibal downstairs, and it was time to get up.

At breakfast with Anthony, he showed her and Sarah the wedding invitation he had drafted on his computer. "What do you think?"

Anthony Bartlett-Brown and Patricia Anderson
request the pleasure of your company
at the Manor House, Summerfield
18 December - 7:00 p.m.
for a Christmas Feast,
to celebrate their engagement.

&

At St Peter's Church, Summerfield
24 December, 4:00 p.m.
for the Blessing of their marriage.
R.S.V.P.

Patricia beamed. "I think it's brilliant! It will be just a small group and they will get it more quickly attached to email. What do you think, Sarah? Is it workable for catering an engagement dinner?"

Sarah nodded, "It is if we start today. It will also be good to help the new staff learn the ropes. They arrive later. Once they settle in, I will start organizing."

Patricia tilted her head, questioning, "New staff?"

"I'll let Sarah explain about staff and send the invitations out later." Anthony glanced at his watch and shut the laptop. "David is driving me to an appointment at the hospital and we are having lunch in Oxford."

He stopped to kiss Patricia's head in passing.

"I will not be here when you get back." She smiled at his anxious look. "Sweetheart, don't fuss. I am fine and need to go back to Halfmoon Cottages to pack everything. I will stay the night there with Sophie and get lots done. I promise I will call you later."

A horn sounded, and Anthony departed. Patricia poured more tea for Sarah and herself. "New staff?"

"I want to take early retirement after Christmas, but did not want to tell anyone until we found a suitable live-in couple. I interviewed and did a day's trial with two couples. Both were excellent, but Anthony preferred Lorenzo, who will be his caregiver and driver. They are originally from Portugal and Maria, Lorenzo's partner, is an experienced cook and housekeeper. They are on a three-month trial, and I will train them before I leave."

Sarah sipped her tea. "Are you sure about marrying Anthony?"

The smile spread across Patricia's face. "Yes. I had time in that crypt to focus on what is important. Being with Anthony is truly what I want now."

"I'm glad, because he adores you."

Patricia gazed out the window. "Life is brief and I appreciate him so much. If you would help me understand his medication, hopefully, we will have some time. But what about you? Talk about me keeping secrets, I did not know you were thinking of retiring. It has been lovely, becoming closer friends, and I hope you are not going far away."

"I would like to stay in Summerfield, but there is nothing at all to rent. I wonder if I could be your new tenant for Number 2, Halfmoon Cottages?"

Astonished, Patricia put down the cup. "That's a fabulous idea, but would you want to live there, after those horrible people?"

"I loved the cottage before they moved in, and the terrible memories are all yours. It is as good as new again and I should love to have a dog. Most landlords do not allow pets, but I know you would be okay with that. I could still look after Sophie and Hannibal while you go on your honeymoon. I could still sing with the choir. Obviously, you will use a rental agency this time, but could I apply for the tenancy?"

Patricia chuckled, "On the advice of a close friend, I am using Banbury Rental Agency, and I would love to have you live there as the new tenant! How exciting! Could you also help me choose someone for Number 1? I have lost my confidence in judging people. I know from bitter experience that the person needs to be compatible with their neighbor!"

Sarah smiled. "I would love to help you choose. Would you consider Audrey? Her daughter and grandson moved permanently to Oxford, and the Council allocated her house to another family. She has a month to move out and is worried sick."

* * *

With Sophie in the back of the Morris 1000, Patricia chugged down Church Lane and parked on the big letters in front of the cottages. She unlocked the door of Number 2 feeling apprehensive, but Sarah was right. Everything was pristine and she would call the rental agency tomorrow.

Patricia packed boxes in her own cottage until it began to get dark. "Come on, Soph, we need one last log fire to glow in the grate while we pack the books. It's only four o'clock, but goodness, the wind is cold tonight!"

She headed down the path with the log basket. Sophie dashed ahead but stopped, her nose pointing at the old pigsty. Her tail wagged, but Patricia pulled the mobile phone from her pocket, thumb poised over the alarm to Anthony.

"If someone is in the woodstore, please come out."

She was astonished when the Goth Boy emerged, crumpled and filthy. His black hair showed lighter at the roots, and the floppy bit was too long. Head down, he muttered, "I shut you in. I panicked, but when I saw your dog running away, I calmed down. I came back to let you out, but the man had already found you. I'm sorry."

He pushed the hair back to reveal ash-white skin with freckles. His eyes were too old for a boyish face. "I didn't have anywhere to go, so I came here."

Sophie nuzzled his leg, and the Goth Boy collapsed on the low wall. He stroked her head, murmuring quietly, and Patricia's heart softened because Sophie trusted him.

"Why didn't you go with your family?"

"They don't want me. I go to the ponies every day and come here at night, now that I can't get under the church."

"But how did you get in, and how did you get the key to the crypt?"

The boy shrugged. "Easy, there's a loose window. I am good with tech stuff and ran the CCTV tape. I saw him teach you."

His head bent over Sophie, as if he would fall asleep any moment. Patricia knew that feeling but pressed on. "But you didn't steal the cross."

"You can't eat gold. I took a food box and had the peanut butter with cookies."

"Weren't you afraid, sleeping down there?" Patricia shuddered.

The Goth Boy lifted his head, "Dead people don't hurt anyone. Please, could you help me? They are looking for me and I don't have anywhere to hide."

Patricia looked up the path to her warm kitchen. She had thought she was an excellent judge of people, but his mother had tricked her. "Are you hungry? Or, since I have grandkids, is that a stupid question?"

The shadow of a grin crossed the boy's thin face.

Sophie trotted with him as Patricia led the way. "Shoes off."

She sat him at the table while she warmed up a can of chicken soup. She made toast, and he watched, elbows spread wide with hands holding back his hair. Patricia loaded grated cheese on the soup and put a plate of buttered toast next to the bowl. "Okay, all yours."

The boy devoured everything in record time. Patricia gave him a big mug of tea with three cookies and sat down opposite him. "If you could answer a few more questions, I could call a youth shelter in Oxford and see if they can take you. I am Patricia Anderson, but I don't know your name."

"It's Matthew Smithers, Matt to Gran, my grandma. But everyone calls me Ginger."

Patricia glanced at his hair.

"It's red. I hate it and dye it black, but they still call me Ginger."

"Could your father help you?"

"He took off when I was born and never paid child support. Mum took Tracey, but left me with Gran, her mum."

Matt whistled softly through his teeth. Sophie went to him and rested her head on his knee, exactly as she did with Patricia. He caressed her head with a dirty hand. "Gran brought me up, but she died when I was fifteen, two years ago. I tried to survive on my own, but I had no money. Mum gave me some when Darren was not around. But Tracey's boyfriend threatened us, unless I delivered stuff for him."

Food had given the boy enough energy to talk. "We came here, and I found the ponies. I tried to get away from him, but he told me I needed to do more deliveries, or they would set fire to the stables."

Patricia remembered the angry eyes of the man in the kitchen, and Robert had spoken of drug dealers using school kids. "Are you talking about county lines drug running?"

Matt shrank and looked around. "Don't say it out loud or he will kill me. I am not kidding you. Sometimes, I think I would be better off dead."

Patricia had almost decided to take him in but had one important question, "Do you use drugs?"

The boy shivered. "No, I got allergic reactions to anything they gave me and vomited everywhere. I'm the useful wimp who doesn't steal to get a fix."

"That's lucky if you want to be free of them. Where were you when the police raided here?"

"Out delivering. Then I got the keys to under the church and disappeared. But they are looking for me. My dream is to work with horses."

Matt's face was ashen, and Patricia stood up. "Okay, would you like a shower? You can sleep on the couch tonight and I will make calls for you in the morning."

Tears came to his eyes. "You are like Gran. She said she took in waifs and strays."

"You are certainly one of those!"

Patricia showed him the downstairs shower, and found two black towels in the laundry closet. "Paul, my son, likes black too. I have some of his clothes upstairs and will put them on the couch with some bedding. I also have some pajamas, but they were my husband's. You won't mind that, will you?"

"Are you divorced?"

"No, he died about five years ago. I could not throw his things away."

The boy hesitated, "Do you have scissors and a razor?"

Patricia froze.

"If I shave my head and wear different clothes, maybe I can get away."

* * *

Patricia took Ron's and Paul's things from a box in the landing closet. She twisted the wedding ring she had worn for over forty years and then took it off. It was thinner than when Ron put it on her finger.

She got some tissue paper from her bedroom and carefully wrapped the ring, kissing it before slipping it into an envelope of family photographs in the box. Gathering the clothes, sheets, blankets, and a pillow, Patricia took them downstairs. Water ran in the shower, and Sophie sat by the door, her head cocked to one side.

Patricia called Clair from her bedroom. "They have forced him to be a drug mule. He seems to have a moral sense from his grandmother, has stayed clean, and wants to work with horses. Robert watches him with the ponies and Sophie trusts him. Could I bring him to the Stables meeting tomorrow? Maybe we could generate ideas to help him? I think he is in danger."

When she came down again, Matt was deeply asleep. He had one arm wrapped around Sophie and Patricia stroked her head. "You know you're not allowed on the couch; but it's okay, just for tonight. He needs you."

Matt's shaved head had several patches of dried blood on it and he looked like a refugee. Patricia felt hurt for him. "Thank goodness, our son never had to suffer like you."

She checked the doors, took her purse, and went upstairs to call Anthony.

Chapter 24

Breakfast at the cottage with Matt and Anthony was awkward, but after hastily gulping down a gigantic bowl of cereal, Matt took the dogs into the backyard. There was half an hour before they left for the Stables, and Anthony searched databases on his laptop.

"All good. Matthew Smithers will be eighteen in August and has no police file."

Patricia came to look over his shoulder. "How would you feel, if I got him a work placement, and managed his paperwork, until he can become independent?"

Anthony reached up to touch her hand. "I would support whatever you want, my love, but I need to ask him how he got into the crypt."

"He told me." Patricia repeated what Matt had said and Anthony looked impressed. "He is not stupid. That cross has an electronic trace on it. I will fix the window and change the combination to the safe."

He watched Matt playing with the dogs. "It was also sensible to shave his head, lose the earrings and take the bone out of his nose."

Patricia laughed. "It was a fashion accessory, not a bone!"

"Whatever. He stands a better chance of honest employment without it."

* * *

Later, Patricia and Anthony sat at the table in the Stables Training Room with the others and Matt waited outside.

Audrey was incredulous. "You trust that Goth Boy after he shut you in the crypt?"

"He thought I was someone else. He came back to let me out but saw Anthony rescue me. I made a naïve mistake with his mother. I am asking your advice about this young man. I see his potential and the enormous challenges ahead. He is like all the kids who come here, just with unique challenges. Helping kids with limitations to live better lives is what Summerfield Stables does. Could we get one street kid out of danger this Christmas?"

Robert had been a police officer and David, a military instructor. Both had extensive experience with young men.

Robert turned to Clair, "I've watched him in the field, and he is good with the ponies. We could try him here for a few days and see how it goes."

David nodded, "I could share supervision with Robert."

"Then we will give him a chance." Clair smiled at Patricia, "Bring him in."

"Thank you!" Patricia jumped to her feet. "We have been calling him Goth Boy, but his proper name is Matt. He has naturally auburn hair, but dyed it when the others bullied him. He is desperate to change his identity and get away, so he's shaved his head."

The youngster who followed Patricia back into the room looked younger than seventeen years. His jeans hung off him and he twisted Patricia's Summerfield Stables cap awkwardly in his hands. Light bounced off the shaved scalp and his ears stuck out like wings. He was unrecognizable as the Goth Boy.

Clair went to greet him, holding out a mug. "Welcome, Matt, I am Clair. Patricia said you take milk and two sugars in your coffee. Please sit down and you can put your cap back on."

Matt pulled on the cap and took the coffee. "Thank you."

Clair settled him at the table and David took over. "Hi, I'm David. This is Audrey, who runs our office, and Robert, who manages the Stable Yard. We'd like to know why you want to work with horses."

Matt cradled his coffee mug in both hands. The silence seemed to go on too long, but he stole a look at Patricia and gained confidence. "I've always loved horses, ever since I was a kid and only saw them in pictures. When Gran died, I went on the road. I did anything to stay alive, but when I found the ponies…"

He paused, searching for words…"it felt like… I was home. When I was younger, I wanted to join the mounted police, but was never allowed to take any exams."

Clair leaned on the back of her chair, "Would you like a trial with Robert in the stable yard?"

Matt's face lit up. "Yes!"

"We start early, work long days, and sometimes nights. Are you up for that?"

"You mean, am I too small?" Matt sounded as if others had asked him this before. "People think I'm weak, but Gran said we come from Welsh miners. All her family were small. I am strong and I work hard."

Clair smiled. "You remind me of Granddad. He was small and wiry like you. He worked with horses all his life."

Audrey took the car keys from her purse. "I have some clothes and things at home that might fit you. I'll be back soon."

Robert considered the young man in the Stables cap. "Can you start today?"

Matt immediately stood up.

Everyone laughed as Robert motioned him to sit down. "Finish your coffee, and then we will go. The Volunteers at the Stables know Patricia. She told us that some unpleasant people might be looking for you. To avoid any confusion, your name is Matt Anderson. You are a distant relative of Patricia's, joining us for Work Experience. Okay?"

Matt's eyes widened and looked to Patricia. "Thanks."

Robert pointed upward, "I've only got a one-bed apartment up there, so you get the couch."

Audrey came in and heaved a large plastic bag onto the table. "My grandson grew out of these, and there's a pair of short riding boots that might fit."

"Cool!"

Matt carefully separated out black jeans and a black T-shirt. "Could I leave these with you? I do not want to wear black anymore."

Robert stood up, carrying his coffee mug. "Okay, let's go. The first horse I will teach you to groom is Winston, my ex-police horse."

With a grin for Patricia, Matt picked up his mug, slung Audrey's bag over his shoulder and followed Robert out.

Patricia gave Clair a hug before she headed to the arena for her next class. "Thank you so much for giving him a chance."

Patricia sat down to wait for Anthony, who was speaking with David.

David called, "See you later, Patricia!"

He and Audrey gathered the last coffee mugs and waved goodbye. They went out talking about invoices, and the door to the Training Room swung shut behind them. Anthony sat down beside her. "Well done! That was a successful meeting, and I told David that, if you agree, I will sponsor Matt's training costs."

Patricia gave him a kiss. His skin smelled of olive soap from Kalamata. "You are such a kind man! I don't have the funds to do that."

"I'm glad we have a quiet moment because I wanted to

show you this." Anthony brought a small box out of his jacket pocket. It was covered in faded red velvet and inside was an exquisite diamond, set in a circle of small sapphires. "It was Mother's, but not her engagement ring. It is Victorian, and I remember her wearing it. I would love you to have it as our engagement ring, but I need you to be honest. If it's not to your taste, we will go to Oxford right now and find another."

Patricia cupped her hands around his to hold the ring box. "It is gorgeous and even more precious because it belonged to your mother. I have small hands, so it may fit without resizing."

Anthony looked intently into her eyes. "Before I put it on, did you mean it when you said you would marry me? I'm afraid you said yes because I rescued you from the crypt."

Patricia's face crinkled with laughter. "Dearest Anthony, if Jim had got me out of the crypt, I would not have said yes to marriage! My heart changed when I was shut in there."

She squeezed his hand. "Ours is a different love from the love I had with Ron. It is different from my love for Paul, my grandchildren, or Sophie. You are my dearest friend, and I prayed you would find me in the crypt. I want us to be married for the rest of our lives."

This cheered Anthony, and he took her left hand in his. "I'm sorry I can't go down on one knee, but if I do, I will never get up again! Darling Patricia, would you do me the honor of becoming my wife?"

"Yes, I will."

He slipped the ring onto her finger, and it fit perfectly.

Anthony's lips touched hers and she kissed him back. She did not feel a romantic, storybook explosion. It was a tender kiss, the nicest kiss ever. "I'm so glad Tim will conduct a Blessing Service for us at St Peter's. Since I am dedicated to serving God, I presume I can still work there after we are married?"

"I don't know about that." Anthony stood up, frowning. "We'll need to ask the verger."

Patricia laughed, and they walked out of the Training Room arm in arm. "You are a tease and I am ravenously hungry. We could go to the Potlatch Inn and I will buy you an engagement lunch of chicken in a basket of crispy fries. Then we must finish the Christmas Food Bank boxes with Audrey."

* * *

It was too cold to pack boxes in the church, so they moved everything to Patricia's cottage. Audrey made happy little sounds as she moved around the kitchen. "I can't believe you are leasing this cottage to me. I know you could get a higher rent."

"Ha! I learned the hard way that good tenants are worth their weight in gold. The Banbury office will manage everything with you, but your rent will always be the same as the Council rate."

Patricia lined a box with Christmas wrapping paper and light flashed from her ring.

"May I see?"

Patricia held out her hand.

"Congratulations, it is beautiful."

Audrey glanced over her shoulder at Anthony clearing out the 4 x 4. "If I had a gentleman caller, could he stay sometimes?"

Patricia grinned. "The cottages have two bedrooms and the Tenancy Agreements specifies four people maximum. Your daughter and grandson can stay too."

"And you know I've got two cats?"

"Audrey, if you had two hippos, you would be a better choice than my first tenants!"

They collapsed in laughter, and Audrey blushed. "I am older than Jim, but we are both widowed and like cats. It might work."

Patricia looked down at her ring. "Who knows what works? Good luck, and we will see you both at the engagement dinner."

"Jim said, would you like him to pick the Christmas roses for your wedding bouquet?"

"Tell him, thank you, I would love that!"

Audrey counted the boxes. "Okay, eleven Summerfield families get food, toiletries, and an equal share of the money we collected for them."

Anthony came in and picked up a box. "Ready to go?"

Patricia took another and followed him down the path. It was 6:00 p.m., dark and cold. "Thanks for letting me off from the delivering, guys. I have the kitchen to pack before the moving men come tomorrow."

They loaded boxes in the light streaming down the path, and Patricia hurried back inside with Sophie. While Audrey carried the last box out, Anthony pulled Patricia behind the front door and kissed her soundly. "I heard what Audrey said about Jim and am glad he has forgiven you."

Grinning wickedly, he lifted her hand to kiss their ring. "I got the girl, but maybe he will still get the cottage with Audrey in it?"

"Shhhh! She might hear you. Don't be so cynical!"

"Me! Cynical?" Anthony hooted and released her. "I'm the romantic one, remember? Get cracking with the packing, and we'll be back as soon as possible."

Patricia shut the door, and Sophie settled under the kitchen table. How strange to be packing up to leave Halfmoon Cottages. But wonderful to think that Sarah and Audrey would move in and enjoy them.

Suddenly, Patricia thought of Matt and called Robert. "How is he doing?"

"He learns fast and, interestingly, whistles through his teeth when he is grooming, just like Ted. David thinks Matt might make a jockey. He is calling an old buddy who owns a racing stable in Newmarket."

"Could I take Matt to the equestrian store during his lunch hour tomorrow? If you tell me what he needs, I can get things as his Christmas gift."

Robert dictated, and Patricia wrote a list. She clicked off the phone, feeling optimistic about Matt. She was increasingly anxious about Paul. It was two days since Anthony had sent the wedding invitations. Patricia added a loving note to Paul and Eve, but there had been no reply. Were they still angry with her? Should she call? She would ask Anthony when he returned.

Sophie came from under the table and stretched as Patricia finished packing the kitchenware. "Sarah has nothing, so all the furniture will go next door. Audrey is bringing all her stuff and I will ask the movers to take all our things to the Manor House. We can sort it after Christmas."

Powerful headlights swept across the front window, and Patricia glanced at the clock. "Too early to have finished. They must have forgotten something."

At the window, she shaded her eyes and exclaimed with joy. She rushed out to hug Paul. "Oh, my dear. I'm so glad to see you!"

He hugged her back and held her at arm's length. "I'm happy to see you too, Mum. But what have you been up to? You swear you will never marry again, and I was driving over to invite you to come on vacation with us—but you are getting married!"

Sophie jumped around them, and Paul bent to pat her. Patricia shivered, "Come inside, before we freeze! Would you like hot tea?"

"Please, and congratulations! Show me your ring. Oh yes, that is lovely. We are looking forward to meeting

Anthony, and the girls are excited that you will live in a Manor House."

Patricia could not help but boast a little as she plugged in the kettle. "At present, Anthony's father is Sir George Bartlett-Brown. One day, he will be Sir Anthony and I will be Lady Patricia."

She turned to him, her face serious. "But I will never forget your dad or our years together as a family. I have his ring safe for you or one of the girls later."

Paul squeezed her hand. "I know you will not forget, any more than I will. Your life is not over and it is great you have found someone special. We will be at your Blessing Service on Christmas Eve and want you to bring Anthony to lunch on Christmas Day. We fly to Hawaii the next day."

"Hawaii?" Patricia paused in gathering the tea things. "Just you and Eve?"

He shook his head. "The entire family—Eve's mum and dad as well."

The tea was abandoned as Patricia climbed onto a stool next to him. "How did all this happen? You haven't had a vacation in years."

"The last time I was here I went home furious and told Eve what you said. I got a wake-up call. Our marriage had been drifting, and she wanted to talk about a separation. I asked her what I could do to prove I still cared, and Eve proposed a family holiday, plus less travel next year. I have spoken with my business partners and we are taking on a new consultant for the work in China. The family will fly to Hawaii on the 26th, but without you, Mum."

Patricia beamed. "This is wonderful. The girls will love it, particularly if they leave their phones behind."

Patricia's eyes twinkled. Paul glanced at her to see if she was serious and laughed as he got down from his stool. "Fat chance of that! I hate to be always rushing away, Mum, but I wanted to see you, and not just call or email. Eve and I are going out for a romantic dinner tonight and I must not be late."

They walked down the hall with Paul's arm around Patricia. He paused at the front door. "Are you sure you're okay with getting married?"

"More than okay and I so appreciate you coming over. Anthony is a special man and I know you will like him. Just to avoid embarrassment, could you tell Eve and the girls that he has Parkinson's disease? He sometimes gets tremors in his hand."

"Will do," Paul waved as he jogged to his car. "Take care and I'll see you soon!"

Chapter 25

Patricia and Anthony spent the morning of the engagement dinner finishing the Christmas decorations at the Manor House. Sarah had supervised Jim with putting up holly and ivy. Three healthy Christmas trees came from the Duke's estate.

Lorenzo, the new handyman, helped Jim to set up two smaller Christmas trees, one on either side of the front door in the pillared porch. It needed four men to pull the biggest fir tree along the polished oak floor of the hallway horizontally. The massive pot came first, and the trunk next, its branches tightly wrapped in burlap. They hoisted it carefully to its vertical position, standing at the bottom of the Grand Staircase. Secured to the post at the base of the stairs, and unwrapped, the tree seemed to breathe and stretch two floors up to touch the cherubs on the painted ceiling.

Sarah decorated the smaller trees on the porch, but the gigantic tree was special. Anthony told them where to find the boxes of family decorations. Patricia and Sarah held up different ornaments, and Anthony pointed to where each was traditionally hung on the tree. "I shall assume a management role, sit in my armchair, conserve energy for the dinner, and issue orders!"

In Parkinson's terminology, Anthony mostly had 'on days.' The medications worked, and he felt fine. There was an occasional 'off day' when symptoms surfaced, and the meds needed adjustment. He had regular appointments at the Oxford hospital and was part of a research program, which gave him a support group of fellow Parkinson's pioneers.

Patricia held up a little Christmas stocking, nine inches long, handmade in purple velvet, sewn with gold thread. Anthony held out his hand for it in happy recognition. "My mother made this for me when I was five years old."

He turned it over and showed her tiny embroidered letters, *Anthony.*

"All those years ago." Patricia heard the wonder in his voice and recalled another of Ted's old country sayings. *The way a man respects his mother is the way he will also respect his wife.*

Yesterday, Lorenzo had twisted tiny white stars on transparent electric cables all around the trunk of the tree and through many of its branches. When the decorations were all placed, Anthony switched on the lights. The tree blazed with Christmas cheer and they all applauded.

Anthony pointed upward, "You can stand on the top landing now, Sarah, and place the angel as our crowning glory."

* * *

Sarah and Maria were doing last-minute preparations for the engagement dinner, and Patricia carried a tray with sandwiches to Anthony's sitting room. "I will have a quick lunch and be off to go get Matt."

Winter sunlight slanted in through the long windows, and outside, the distant hills were misty blue. Rose bushes had bare, cut stems but inside, Sarah had filled Anthony's elegant Chinese vases with golden chrysanthemums. Lamps with yellow silk shades lit the floor-to-ceiling shelves that held thousands of books. The room was warm and comfortable with carpets from Persia on the polished oak floorboards, and a collection of family photos on Anthony's desk.

"I shall spend the afternoon with my legs stretched toward the log fire, dogs in their beds, reading *The Times*."

Patricia kissed him. "I will leave you in bliss and be back soon."

He smiled up at her. "Drive carefully, I love you."

"Love you too, rest up for tonight."

* * *

It was great to see Matt waiting in the Stables parking lot. He looked like a different young man wearing jeans that fit, with a Summerfield Stables fleece jacket. He had personalized the visor of his own Stables cap, so his ears were less prominent.

He was bursting to talk about what Robert had already taught him. "I had my first riding lesson with Clair on Winston, and it was ace! The best news is that David got me a place at his friend's racing stables in Newmarket! I start as a trainee groom after Christmas. David says that my size and weight will qualify me for the jockey program. The stable where I will train has been at the center of thorough-bred horseracing since 1667! How about that?"

Matt's eyes sparkled. They drove to the horse store and had fun buying all his riding gear. Patricia took him into the 'formal' section of the shop. "I want you to choose something casual but fashionable for tonight."

When they returned to the parking lot, Matt piled the shopping bags into the back of the car. He jumped into the passenger seat of the Morris 1000 as Patricia started the engine.

"My granddaughters will be there this evening. Charlotte is fifteen and Amber is thirteen, so it will not be formal, just some fabulous food with a few family members and friends. Robert said he will bring you with him and it will probably be best not to mention your family or Halfmoon Cottages."

Matt grinned. "Right! I have better things to talk about now."

Patricia had plugged her phone into the speaker between the front seats. She often listened to audio books as she drove, and now it pinged with a text. "Could you look at that for me, please, Matt? It might be Anthony."

"It is Robert. He says, 'Urgent. If you are driving, please pull over and call me.'"

Patricia did that and Robert picked up on the second ring. His voice came through the speaker. "An unpleasant visitor just left us. He said he was Ginger Smithers' father. Ginger is apparently a thief, an underage runaway, and wanted by the police. He gave me his number and said if we saw Ginger around, we should call him, to avoid further trouble."

The blood drained from Matt's face. Robert's voice was calm. "It is all rubbish, but we acted as if we were grateful for the information. David called his friend in Newmarket and offered to bring Matt today. That pleased them, as they are short-staffed and have racing on the 26th. Can you get back pronto? David has your dinner tonight and needs to be there for his brother, so I will drive Matt to Newmarket."

Patricia felt the same anxiety that she saw on Matt's face.

Robert continued, "Drive around the back of the barn. I'll load Matt's stuff into the Jeep and take him out through the fields. We can join the Oxford Road from a field gate. They may have gone, but watch out as you come through the village."

"We're on our way now. Please could you tell Anthony?"

Patricia started the engine and patted Matt's arm. "Don't worry, it will be okay."

He was silent, but as they entered Summerfield, he choked. Three male figures dressed in black stood talking to youngsters by the steps of the War Memorial.

"They're here. They've found me."

Patricia felt a burn of rage. Such evil people thought they could take a boy and use him like this! But there was no other way to the Stables, and she must drive past them.

"They have not found you. You are Matt Anderson, a member of my family. Turn on the radio." Patricia held the steering wheel with one hand and pulled a thick wedge cushion from beneath her. She needed it to give her height to see over the steering wheel. "Sit on this."

Matt looked puzzled, but did as he was told.

Patricia continued driving at her normal slow speed. "Ginger Smithers went to London with his mother. You are heading to work at one of the top racing stables in the country. Turn your face to me now and laugh loudly. Just act it, Matt! NOW!"

The old green car chugged past the War Memorial. A small, white-haired woman was driving, and a tall guy faced her. He wore a jacket with *Summerfield Stables* written across the back, with a matching baseball cap. They were laughing, and pop music blared all around them.

Safely past, Patricia looked in the rearview mirror. "A quick glance at us and they have gone back to chatting up the girls."

She turned down Stables Lane and pulled into the first turnout. "Whew!"

They both burst into genuine laughter and Matt took off his cap to wipe his sweating scalp. "You are awesome!"

"You are too." Patricia started down the lane again. "You survived two dangerous years. It is Christmas, and you deserve a new start. We will all come to watch Matt Anderson ride his first race at Newmarket."

* * *

When she got back to the Manor House, Patricia had a much-needed cup of tea with Anthony. "The ghouls were still by the War Memorial on the way back, but Matt escaped with Robert. Before he went, we threw his mobile phone into the slurry pit by the dung pile. They won't be able to track it in there!"

After relating all the details, she stood and gathered her things. "I am going to my room for a relaxing soak in the tub, sweetheart, until it is time to dress for dinner. Come, Sophie."

Patricia climbed the Grand Staircase by the magnificent tree and looked at faces in the Bartlett-Brown ancestral portraits.

She stopped by Florence's portrait and looked into her sapphire blue eyes. "Thank you for my beautiful ring."

The moving men had stacked everything from the cottage in Patricia's suite. She opened the door to her walk-in closet and stared at the empty rails. Only the outfit for the engagement dinner hung there, so she put her red coat on a hanger next to it. Slipping off her shoes, Patricia sat in the armchair by the window of her bedroom.

Winter dusk rolled in over the countryside and she thought of St Peter's. She and Anthony had agreed with Tim that they would not go back to work until after their honeymoon. Anthony had contracted builders and plumbers to renovate the area by the organ while they were away and replace the horrid bathrooms. "You can start your Mother and Baby group in February, my love."

Patricia sighed with contentment. Before that, there was

their wedding to look forward to! The county Marriage Registry no longer functioned at St. Peter's and the Civil Ceremony would be in Oxford early on the 24th. David and Clair would be their witnesses, and at 4:00 p.m. that afternoon, Tim would conduct the Blessing Service at St. Peter's. St. Mary's choir were coming to sing and were promised a big party at the Manor House after the honeymoon!

Patricia turned on the gold taps in her luxurious bathroom and called Lorenzo. "May I have a small bottle of champagne in my room, please?"

A few minutes later, he brought up a tray with a small ice bucket, a polished glass, champagne, and a dish of olives. Patricia abandoned all worries to a wonderful, long, soak in her tub, with a glass of champagne and soothing music. Wrapped in her long, fluffy robe, she snoozed on the bed until the alarm rang at 5:30 p.m., to dress for dinner.

* * *

Waiting for their guests to arrive, Anthony and Patricia relaxed on the couch by the Christmas tree. The fireplace opposite the Grand Staircase took up half the wall and only had a log fire lit on grand occasions. Sarah usually filled it with flower arrangements.

Today, the enormous, wrought iron fire grate held a section of tree trunk, burning slowly with an occasional waft of apple wood smoke. Lorenzo came in wearing black uniform pants, a white shirt, a black bow tie, and a long, green apron. He settled the log and tidied the grate.

"Thank you, Lorenzo."

He smiled at them and took off his apron as he walked down the hallway to the front door.

Outside, in the dark of a winter evening, the fields glistened with frost. The Manor House porch twinkled with two colorful Christmas trees at the top of the steps. Anthony's citrus wreath hung on the front door, cascading gold ribbons.

Patricia leaned against Anthony's shoulder, gazing into the fire and he took her hand. "Passionate young love is all very well, but this older companionship is lovely and much more peaceful."

She smiled up at him. "We are so lucky to have Sarah and her team doing all the work tonight. Maria is an excellent cook."

"I am uncomfortable being dressed by anyone, but I like Lorenzo. It is a bonus that they both like dogs."

"But I'm glad Sarah wants Sophie and Hannibal with her while we're away."

Anthony sat up carefully, rubbing his forehead and Patricia sat up too. "Do you have a headache? Can I get you something?"

He shook his head. "It was just a twinge; I'll be fine as soon as everyone arrives."

Patricia reached up to kiss him tenderly, her soft, white hair shining like a halo. At last, they heard a '*Rat-a-tat-tat*' on the front door. She jumped up. "They're here!"

Chapter 26

Patricia hurried to join Lorenzo. Now wearing his official, black butler's jacket, he opened the front door and the girls rushed in to hug her.

"Congratulations, Grandma! Hey, you look great!"

"Cool shoes. Can I see your engagement ring?"

"Oh, my goodness, how grown up you both look!"

Patricia's granddaughters wore different colored, sparkly tops with black leggings. Charlotte's was vibrant green and Amber's, a shocking pink. Eve must have helped with their hair and makeup, because they looked so lovely. Patricia noticed Charlotte's smoky grey eyes, so like Ron.

Paul followed the girls in and gave Patricia a big hug. He looked every bit the handsome executive in his best suit. Patricia wore her full-length, black evening skirt with an elegant top in black and silver. It had long chiffon sleeves and a boat neck, which showed off her diamond necklace and earrings. Her silver sandals had low heels and her hair stylist had layer-cut her shining white hair.

Eve stared up at the front of the Manor House. It was a perfect Georgian residence, built in 1830 of warm, honey-colored stone. The large windows and square front porch emphasized its perfect proportions. A giant magnolia tree grew up one side of the wide steps. Paul looked back and called, "Are you coming in, darling?"

Eve walked up the steps like a model and offered Patricia an air kiss. Lorenzo shut the door and took all their coats. Eve wore a short, black designer dress and her diamonds rivaled Patricia's.

Anthony came along the hallway to greet them, looking debonair with his grey hair and neat, white beard. He had on a favorite burgundy velvet jacket, with tailored black slacks, white shirt, and burgundy-spotted bow tie. Patricia introduced everyone, and they all shook hands.

Knowing Patricia's difficulties with her daughter-in-law, Anthony offered Eve his arm and escorted her to the Christmas tree. Patricia took Paul's arm and followed with the girls. At the foot of the Grand Staircase, she left them and turned back to welcome Audrey and Jim, arriving with Clair and David. Jim was more dressed up than she had ever seen him and the lank, grey ponytail had given way to a modern haircut. Well done, Audrey!

He shook hands with Patricia. "I wish you and Anthony all the happiness in the world."

"Thank you! And thanks, too, for picking Christmas roses on the 24th for my bouquet."

"They will be fully out by then. Robert and I have been practicing ringing the bells." He paused, aware that the odd clanging from St Peter's did not resemble the sweetness that pealed from St Mary's. "Don't worry, we'll get it right for your big day."

Audrey hugged Patricia and whispered, "Don't count on it!" and they both laughed. David took her and Jim to introduce them to Paul and Eve.

Amber wanted to see Sophie, so Patricia showed the way downstairs. She had taken the dogs for a short walk and they were on their beds in a corner of the kitchen. Sarah was a guest tonight, but she was there too, doing a last check on dinner with Maria.

When Patricia took Amber and Sarah upstairs again, Lorenzo wheeled in a wine trolley covered with a white cloth. Anthony beamed and held out his hand for Patricia to join him. "Welcome everyone! We have every kind of drink and beverage available, but for this special occasion, I would like to share my collection of antique cocktail glasses with you."

Lorenzo whisked away the cloth to reveal an assortment of rare glasses. Each had a tiny hibiscus flower in the bottom, with a splash of wild hibiscus syrup. From the silver bucket beside them, he took a magnum of champagne, popped the cork, and poured bubbles expertly into each glass. The hibiscus petals slowly unfurled, and the champagne turned a soft pink.

Sarah had hired agency staff. A young man in a waiter's outfit carried glasses to them on a silver platter. Lorenzo made a nonalcoholic version of the cocktail for Anthony, David, and the girls, and Jim had a beer.

When all were served, David lifted his glass. "To my brother Anthony, and his lovely Patricia, many congratulations on your engagement."

Everybody raised their glasses and drank the toast.

"Thank you all." Anthony indicated the magnificent Christmas tree behind him. "It is great to welcome you to the Manor House at this season of the year. David and I were lucky enough to grow up here and have splendid family Christmases. The Bartlett-Browns built this house and left accounts of their Christmas activities. David's mother is American and loved Christmas traditions. She replicated them for us."

David joined in enthusiastically. "We filled the house with friends. There were stories, dancing, and fabulous games, like scary hide-and-seek all over the house! The gifts were spectacular!"

He pointed to a pile of beautifully wrapped Christmas

gifts beneath the tree. "Mother wrote the name of each guest on festive labels. Inside each package was an individually chosen gift to take home at the end of the evening. Anthony and Patricia have done the same for us tonight."

Patricia smiled. She and Anthony had such fun choosing the amazing gifts online, wrapping them, and writing the labels. She moved across the hallway to ask Sarah how long they could wait dinner for Robert. "Twenty minutes more, but no longer, or some dishes will be ruined."

People talked in small groups. Anthony was talking to Clair. Paul was laughing with Jim, and Patricia put her arm round Amber. "I know how much you love horses. Would you like riding lessons as your Christmas gift this year?"

Patricia knew she was being unfair to Eve. If there had been good communication, she would have called to speak with Eve before mentioning this to Amber. Her granddaughter turned enormous blue eyes on her mother. "Mummy, may I?"

Eve surprised Patricia! Not only did she say yes, but also said thank you for the kind offer. Did Eve also sigh and look envious?

On impulse, Patricia said, "If you are driving to Summerfield and waiting for Amber, would you enjoy riding lessons too, as my Christmas gift?"

Eve's face was so much nicer when she smiled. "I would love that! Thank you! Horse riding was something I dreamed of when I was a little girl, but we could never afford it. It would be fun to learn with Amber."

Charlotte looked supremely bored. Her hand rested on her little shoulder purse, as if dying to pull out her phone, and Patricia turned to her. "Anthony and I wondered whether you might like to have your 16th birthday party here? We could pay for it as your Christmas gift and were thinking of driving lessons for your birthday? Your party could be a disco or a ball, whatever you wanted, except, of course, there would be no alcohol."

Now it was Charlotte's turn to light up like a Christmas tree. She turned pleading eyes on her mother, and Eve nodded toward Paul. "Ask Daddy what he thinks."

Amber went with Charlotte to talk to Paul, and it astonished Patricia when Eve hugged her! "Thank you for being such a wonderful Grandma. I'm so happy that you are with Anthony and have a new life in Summerfield."

Patricia drew her to sit down on the couch. "I think it's wonderful you are all going to Hawaii."

The waiter offered them another champagne cocktail and Eve clinked glasses with Patricia. "We are only going because you told Paul some home truths. He came back that day so angry with you, and it gave me an opening to say I wanted a divorce."

Patricia leaned back and sipped her drink, leaving space for Eve to continue.

"I don't want a divorce. I love Paul, but my life had become an endless chore. I could see no end to it. We had long talks. I want to support the girls in everything but Paul is going to travel less and do more at home. I am enrolled on a horticulture course and hope one day to start a business of my own."

"I will drink to that." Patricia clinked glasses as Paul came over to join them. "Would you excuse us for a moment, Mum?"

He offered his hand to Eve. "Come with me, sweetheart. I think you will find Audrey and Jim interesting. They are both keen gardeners and know someone in Summerfield with a horticultural business."

Patricia smiled with contentment, and Clair slid into the space vacated by Eve. "That seemed to go well, and you look happy."

"I am supremely happy." Patricia noticed that Clair did not have a drink. "Would you like a cocktail?"

"No, thanks." Clair grinned at Patricia, and leaned

forward to whisper, "It is early days and we're only telling you and Anthony—I am pregnant."

Patricia reached for Clair's hand and choked on a nose full of bubbles. "I'll whisper; that is WONDERFUL NEWS!"

She looked across the room. David had his back to them, and over his shoulder she read the pure joy on Anthony's face. Tears prickled her eyes. "How miraculous! I marry Anthony on Christmas Eve and am given the gift of a loving man. I also get you as a sister, David as a brother, and a new baby on its way!"

"The baby will be David's and Anthony's heir. We have not decided on a girl's name yet, but if it's a boy, we will call him Ted."

Lorenzo came and spoke quietly to Patricia. He walked to the double doors leading to the dining room and swung them open. "Ladies and Gentlemen, dinner is served."

Patricia crossed the hallway to Anthony, and they led everyone into the beautiful room. In the center of an enormous, circular table, covered with a snowy white cloth stood a many-branched silver candelabra. Thirty candle flames reflected in the gilt mirrors along one wall, and tall vases in the corners of the room flowed with silver-grey grasses. Variegated holly was laid in a circle around the candelabra. It was dark green with cream edges and interspersed with stars in glass lanterns.

They looked for their names on the little place cards, and each of the ten elegant dining chairs had a Christmas cushion on its seat. The gentlemen held chairs out for the ladies and girls to sit. Wait staff held chairs for the gentlemen. Anthony and Patricia sat next to each other nearest the door. Eve was on Anthony's other side, then Paul and the girls. Next came Clair, then David, Audrey, Jim, and Sarah. In between her and Patricia, the seat was empty.

Robert arrived, just as the staff carried in silver platters with the starters. He waved to everyone and sat down. "I saw Matt settled before I left Newmarket. On the way, I suggested he take the labels off his new gear. He re-packed everything into an old army kitbag David gave him. We stopped for coffee at a motorway service station, and I bought him a new phone as my Christmas gift."

Robert smiled up at a waiter. "I'd like melon, please."

He turned back to Patricia, shaking out his napkin. "I found the Yard Manager when we arrived. He immediately gave Matt a new cap and fleece in their racing colors, so I brought ours home again. Another groom was appointed as Matt's mentor and took him off to see the yard. Matt will live in a dormitory with three other trainees."

"What about food?"

"They have a cafeteria where everyone eats. Only the owner knows Matt's true story, so when I said goodbye, I quietly warned Matt to keep quiet about his past. I think he will. I left him at evening mucking out with his mentor, surrounded by racehorses, and loving it. He said he would call you tomorrow."

Patricia took his hand and squeezed it. "I cannot thank you enough. That young man already has a piece of my heart."

Robert grinned as he looked appreciatively at his starter. "We all want him to succeed."

Anthony leaned in, "Is everything okay?"

Patricia smiled at him as she started her extravagant prawn cocktail. "Yes! I'll tell you the details later, but it looks like we got him out just in time."

Sarah and Maria had created a fabulous feast. After the starters, the vegan main course for Eve and Charlotte was roast pumpkin with cranberry stuffing, or a festive vegan log. For everyone else, there was Beef Wellington, glazed local ham, or wild Atlantic salmon, poached with spinach. Glorious organic vegetables from Summerfield market accompanied the mains. Crispy roast potatoes, cauliflower cheese, carrots, Brussels sprouts, creamy mashed potatoes, and delicious gravy, meat, or vegan. When everyone was served and began eating, there were murmurs of content all around the room.

Patricia looked around. Jim related a tale to a laughing Audrey, while Clair and David held hands beneath the tablecloth. Amber was telling Paul about ponies, and he shook his head at Charlotte as she slid her phone onto the table. Patricia was pleased to see it disappear again. Anthony told Eve the history of the Manor House and, pretending to listen, Patricia watched Sarah and Robert from the corner of her eye.

To thank her for all her support and caring for Sophie while they were away, Patricia had taken Sarah to the hair salon. Sarah said once she would love to change her hair color, but did not have the courage. Tonight, instead of grey hair held back in a clip, Sarah had a shoulder-length bob in a lovely soft blonde color. She was wearing an attractive, fitted dress, with earrings and matching necklace. She looked more like forty than fifty. Robert had returned to the Stables in time to shower and change. He wore a crisp, white, open-neck shirt with grey chinos and a dark blue, tailored jacket.

Might something happen between them?

Patricia hoped so. They were both lovely people.

The desserts stunned them! There was cherry and vodka trifle served in circular cut-glass dishes. Maria had frosted a dark chocolate Christmas log with silver balls and made individual frozen delights with fresh peaches and home-made ice cream.

Parkinson's meds do not mix well with sugar, so Anthony enjoyed a slice of crumbly Cornish cheddar, with walnuts and spicy carrot chips.

When they could eat no more, David tapped his fork against his glass and looked to Patricia. In the silence, she leaned forward and smiled to see all their faces.

"Thank you all for coming tonight and making our happiness complete."

She took Anthony's hand and smiled at him. "Finding a loving partner later in life has brought us such blessings and we look forward to lots of adventures. We especially thank Sarah, Maria, and Lorenzo for making our engagement dinner a dream come true."

Everyone applauded. Lorenzo and Maria were standing in the doorway and looked pleased as they left quietly to set up coffee in the sitting room.

Anthony stood up. "My turn to thank you all for being here to celebrate our engagement."

He walked around his chair and leaned on the back. "It is great to meet Patricia's family tonight and a big thank you to David and Clair for all their support."

He looked down at Patricia and his eyes said he adored her. Patricia smiled back at him, thinking of everything that had brought them together.

Anthony continued, "I am the luckiest man in the world. When I came back to Summerfield, Patricia was busily transforming St Peter's, so I got busy, getting in her way."

Everybody laughed with him. "I think you know that I spent a long and seemingly successful life in London, thinking that one day, someone would walk in and change everything. But no one came. I returned home and thought everything was over. Then a Church of England verger in a black robe captured my heart."

Anthony walked around the chair and held out his hand to her. "Dearest Patricia, I love so much about you. Your fabulous blue eyes and the way your smile lights…"

Something went dreadfully wrong.

Anthony froze, like a toy whose battery has failed. He did not blink, and his eyes were blank.

There was a stunned moment before Patricia jumped up and took his outstretched hand. Anthony's arm was locked, and fearing he would fall, she moved in to support him.

David hurried to his other side. "Clair, will you call an ambulance? Sarah, please will you take everyone into the sitting room?"

Patricia looked at Anthony's face and saw the knight in St. Peter's church, frozen in stone beneath his canopy.

Chapter 27

Anthony lay on a hospital gurney waiting to go into the operating theater. He wore a sterile white gown and they had covered his beard, but not his head.

Patricia held his hand and bent close in her gown and mask. "I love you."

Eyes closing with sedation, Anthony whispered, "I love you too."

The orderly pushed the gurney on silent wheels through the swinging doors and Patricia stared as they quietly shut behind him. They say that true love hits you like a thunderbolt, but she had never felt it until now. Removing her protective equipment, Patricia put it in the bin, washed her hands, and stumbled along the corridor.

At the Nursing Station, David stood talking to a doctor. She was in her thirties and wore scrubs, the pale blue top and draw-string slacks of a surgeon. Her hair was all hidden beneath a sterile cap, and a mask hung on its string around her neck.

"Dr. Adebayo, this is my brother's fiancée, Mrs. Anderson." They shook hands. "Patricia, Dr. Adebayo is one of Anthony's specialists."

The doctor had a lovely smile, but she looked tired.

"I run the Parkinson's Research Project and Anthony's medications have become progressively less effective. But we could not increase the dosage because of adverse side effects. I have finished my operating list but my colleague is in surgery with Anthony now."

Patricia understood now that Anthony had shared little of his Parkinson's treatment. The hospital was a different world that Patricia had entered with Ron but had avoided since he died. Anthony had returned from hospital appointments, enthusing about time spent with his brother in Oxford and assuring her that all was progressing well. But her denial was over. If they were to marry, she would be back in the hospital world.

Dr. Adebayo's pager vibrated, and she glanced at it before continuing, "Parkinson's freezing leads to increased falls. Anthony signed the release for DBS, Deep Brain Stimulation, in case it became necessary. His surgery will take four to five hours."

"What are the risks?"

"Our Patient Rating for this procedure is 92.5%, and we have proof it reduces freezing; but there is a small possibility of a bleed on the brain or a stroke. The worst-case scenario is paralysis. But with no complications, Anthony will be home in three days."

She turned to David. "You asked to see the operating theater from the Student Viewing Room and Anthony previously signed the consent. I can take you before I go off duty."

Dr. Adebayo led them up a side staircase to a soundproof room. Two rows of seats faced a one-way window and Patricia's eyes filled with tears as she looked down at the still figure on the operating table.

A surgical team was completing preparations, and Dr. Adebayo muted the sound on the console. "Anthony is part of our research project, and all the patients in that group have surgery videoed for teaching purposes."

Patricia was startled when the lights went out below and Dr, Adebayo reassured her. "That is normal; they need intense light on the area of surgery."

But David was concerned and touched Patricia's arm. "I know you want to support Anthony, but wouldn't you be more comfortable in the Waiting Room? I am familiar with medical procedures and can tell you about it later."

"Maybe you're right."

Dr. Adebayo opened the door. "The Waiting Room is down the stairs and to the left. Someone will come to find you as soon as there is news. If Anthony is recovering well, they will allow you to see him for a few moments."

"Thank you. Goodnight. "

The door closed quietly behind her, and Patricia bowed her head.

When she raised it again, David asked, "Do you believe in prayer?"

Patricia looked toward the one-way window and nodded. "A team of highly trained human beings is working to fix a malfunction in Anthony's brain. But humans did not make the miracle that is his brain. I pray that a Higher Power will watch over him."

David drew her into a gentle hug. "My big brother is a winner. He'll come through this okay."

Patricia went down the stairs to the Waiting Room, and her legs felt shaky. Sarah was waiting there and Patricia was overjoyed. "I am so glad to see you. But it is 2:00 a.m.! You must be exhausted."

Sarah hugged her and poured coffee from the thermos flask into two cups. "I thought you might have a long wait. Clair wanted to come too, but they need her at the Stables. Where is David?"

Patricia told her and sipped hot coffee while Sarah took a thermos and sandwiches to David in the Viewing Room, then returned. "Everyone was in shock when you left in the ambulance. I had Maria make more coffee, and we talked for a while. As they left, I asked them to take their gifts from under the tree because I knew it was what you and Anthony wanted."

Sarah picked up her purse and coat. "I will head home now. Call me when you have any news, please."

"Thank you again." Patricia hugged her. "And for taking care of Sophie and Hannibal."

She was the only person in the Waiting Room and sat back down in the hard chair. The neon glare of the overhead lights made her eyes ache and she shut them.

What if Anthony did not make it?

* * *

Four hours, seven minutes, and many prayers later, David came in and his face said it all.

"Success!" He gratefully took more coffee and another sandwich. "I unmuted the console and listened to that amazing team find the exact location in Anthony's brain. He was unconscious most of the time, but near the end, they brought him around to ask questions. I could hear his voice, then I heard the surgeon say, "Good job, Anthony. We will let you sleep now and see you later.""

A short while later a doctor came to update them. David stayed in the Waiting Room when they allowed Patricia to visit Anthony for two minutes.

She beamed at him from behind her mask. "It's all over, dearest, and you did so well. Everyone at home sends love and David is taking me home. I will be back as soon as they let me. God Bless and sleep well."

Anthony was still lying on his gurney and he gripped her hand. Anesthetic blurred his voice. "I didn't tell you everything. I will understand if you want to break our engagement."

His eyelids fluttered closed, and he slept.

* * *

Later that afternoon, refreshed from deep sleep and a walk with the dogs, Patricia arrived at Anthony's room. He was not in bed but stood by the window in pajamas, robe, and slippers, holding onto a tall metal stand. It had three wheels and a hook at the top; a long tube connected the bag of clear liquid to a port in his arm.

There were dark shadows under his eyes, but he smiled to see her. "The doctor says, keep moving or everything seizes up."

Patricia offered her arm and they went slowly along the corridor and back again before a nurse helped Anthony into bed.

"Dr. Adebayo came in earlier and checked me over. If all is well on her round tomorrow, I can go home."

Patricia sat by the bed and Anthony stared up at the monitors. His voice was depressed. "Eighty percent of my dopamine-producing cells are dead. At some point, I will have more tremors, shuffle, and not be able to communicate. Parkinson's will take over my life and I feel that I must release you from our engagement."

Patricia put her left hand into his and pointed to their engagement ring sparkling in the hospital lights. "I heard you say that before you slept, but my life has changed. I can't switch off loving you because there are difficulties! Whatever comes next, I want to share it with you. Dr. Adebayo told me that the second part of the procedure is in six weeks and suggested we postpone the honeymoon."

Patricia leaned in to kiss him. "She also said there is no

medical reason to postpone our wedding. So, do not think you can wriggle out of marrying me, mister. Our wedding is ON!"

* * *

Patricia was waiting at the front door with the dogs when David brought Anthony home from the hospital. Sophie was free but Hannibal was on his leash and watched the car door open, quivering from nose to tail. He dashed forward and Patricia had to restrain him. He made little sounds, *yip-yip-yip*, like a puppy, and scattered the gravel with massive paws, trying to get near Anthony.

"Hey, Hannibal, good boy! It is great to be home."

Lorenzo brought the dog beds into the sitting room and Hannibal calmed down. Anthony and Patricia had tea there with David. "Clair and I will be here to get you at 10:00 a.m. tomorrow for the Register Office ceremony, and I am your chauffeur to St. Peter's for the Blessing Service at 3:50 p.m."

Anthony's eyes were tender as he looked at his brother. "Thanks for everything. How is Clair doing?"

David grinned as he stood up to leave. "Sick as a dog in the mornings. She says it is the best reason she can think of for vomiting. Rest up, you guys, so you'll be ready for your big day tomorrow."

Patricia walked him to the front door with Sophie. When they returned, Hannibal sat close to Anthony, massive head resting upon his knee. Anthony stroked his tattered ears. "He only tolerated me at first, but he seems glad I am back."

"He has grown to trust you."

"I love him, the mad old idiot." Anthony's hand rested on his dog's head. "It is amazing what happens when a dog gives you his heart."

Patricia sat down and patted Sophie. "Before you came

home, we had some snow and I let them off their leashes to run in the field."

Anthony looked alarmed. "Was that a good idea? What if Sophie had run away?"

"It's okay, I don't think she will run away again. This is our home now. Hannibal will stay because of you, and Sophie will stay because of him.

Anthony leaned in for a soft kiss. "Well, I am staying because of you."

"That's good." Patricia stroked his cheek. "I am staying because of you too."

Chapter 28

At 3:30 p.m. on Christmas Eve, Patricia Anderson stood at the top of the sweeping, Grand Staircase of the Manor House. The enormous Christmas tree shimmered from floor to ceiling, and she held the bannister with one hand as she began to descend.

Patricia loved the swish of her gorgeous, blue velvet cloak and the posy of white Christmas roses in her other hand. She made eye contact with Florence's portrait as she passed and smiled.

Anthony rose from his armchair beside the bright log fire. "You look so beautiful."

His face glowed with love. He offered his hand for the last two stairs, and leaned in to kiss his wife. They had married at the Oxford Registry, but their real wedding was the Blessing Service at St. Peter's this afternoon.

Patricia had asked Sarah to help choose her wedding outfits and saved the medieval-style outfit for now. Anthony carefully raised the wide hood of the cloak to rest upon her hair and frame her face. "The blue is exactly the color of your eyes. What is this fabric?"

"Crushed velvet, with an edging of spun silk."

Beneath the cloak, Patricia wore a calf-length dress in

the same blue, with low-heeled suede boots. Ready to go, Anthony already wore a charcoal overcoat over his suit.

She straightened the collar of his white shirt. "You look so handsome, and I love your tie."

He grinned. "A gift from Sarah. She was the only one who knew the color match."

"Do you have your hat?"

Anthony put on the tweed trilby he liked to wear with the overcoat. Patricia adjusted it and remembered the first time they walked in Potlatch Wood. He had tilted his stockman's hat at a similar jaunty angle, and she had seen loneliness in his eyes. She recognized that the loneliness had been hers too; but it had gone away for both of them now. They were two older people, determined to make the most of every minute.

Anthony offered his arm to walk down the hallway. "I am looking forward to traveling in Greece with my wife."

"It will be wonderful to be in the warm again! But for now, lots of rest and short walks. How is your chest feeling?"

The surgeon had implanted a pulse generator, like a heart pacemaker, under the skin of Anthony's chest. Lorenzo was changing the dressings and Patricia had not seen the site of the surgery.

"The entire area is bruised but Lorenzo says it is healing as it should be."

Patricia stopped to give him the gentlest of hugs but Anthony tensed. "Careful, sweetheart. I don't want a short circuit before everything is connected."

"I am being insanely careful, bionic man! The doctor said you will be able to do much more when they complete the procedure."

They carried on walking and Anthony sighed. "But it's not a cure, is it?"

"No, but you are part of the research project and one day, there will be a cure."

* * *

Oxfordshire lies in the very center of England and rarely has snow, but for the past two days, snowflakes had drifted down, on and off, pushed by a gentle wind. The lawn in front of the Manor House was white, reflecting the golden squares of windows and the flashing colors from the Christmas trees. Stretching away from the garden wall, plowed furrows had the crumbly dark texture of Christmas pudding, dusted with powdered sugar icing. Snow etched the landscape of woods and fields like a sepia drawing. Sophie and Hannibal were warm in the kitchen. Breathing the clean, icy air, Patricia gave thanks for Anthony, their beautiful home, and the professionals who helped them to live comfortably there.

David was waiting with the car and escorted them down the front steps, as the bells of St. Peter's rang out across the village.

Anthony smiled, "Robert and Jim have been practicing."

Patricia leaned up to kiss his cheek. "They are ringing out sadness and ringing in joy."

The white 4 x 4 sparkled. It was clean and empty of Hannibal's dog crate. Clair and David had transformed it into the wedding car with enormous bunches of white ribbon on the side mirrors. More ribbons ran from the radiator to the front doors.

David was Anthony's best man and he bowed as he held the rear door open. "Your carriage awaits!"

With a rhythmic motion, the windshield wipers pushed snow aside in big arcs as he drove them slowly through the village. Parking the 4 x 4 close to the front gate, David offered his hand to Patricia, and then to Anthony, to climb out. "Careful, it is slippery here."

Jim had swept the path and scattered grit. David took them halfway to the church then asked, "Could you wait for two minutes before you follow?"

Golden light streamed from the church. Patricia and Anthony wandered slowly up the path arm in arm, looking at the Christmas card scene of the churchyard in the snow. Patricia pointed up at the tower and they smiled, remembering their first kiss.

Today, St. Peter's welcomed them with joy and love. The bells ceased as they reached the porch and upon the still air came the opening bars of *Silent Night*. Patricia and Anthony stepped inside their church and the harmony of St. Mary's choir singing sent shivers up their spines. The ancient carol rose to the rafters and filled the church.

The interior of the church glowed with hundreds of tea light candles. Clair and the choir members had set them on white saucers along all the windowsills. Tiny flames reflected red, blue, and green in the stained glass and glimmered around the altar. Tiny candles twinkled from every surface of the knight's white tomb and even the little dog seemed to have a sparkle in his eye! Fragrant wreaths of pinecones hung on all the pillars, and Ted's beautiful tree sparkled with lights. Oranges pierced with cloves hung on red ribbons around space heaters placed between the back pews. Warm air circulated, laden with citrus and spices.

Anthony carefully lifted Patricia's hood back from her hair and she helped him take off his hat and coat. Holding hands, they walked to the central aisle. They turned toward the altar, the carol ended, and Audrey smiled from the electric organ. All their choir friends were there, smiling to see them and wearing new, full-length robes of dark green, with white surplices over them.

A lump came into Patricia's throat when she saw the dear faces of her family. Paul, Eve, and the girls were in the front row on one side. Her son had his arm around his wife and Amber leaned against him on the other side. Charlotte stood independently, but love was reflected on all their faces. Patricia and Anthony would be with them for lunch tomorrow in Oxford before they went on vacation. There were family times at the Manor House to look forward to in the future—riding lessons and a birthday party to plan. Best of all, she would share everything with Anthony.

In the front pew opposite them, David and Clair stood with Robert and Sarah. The Bartlett-Brown gold cross gleamed in the center of the altar, flanked by exquisite arrangements of Christmas roses.

Wearing his purple and gold Advent robe, Tim held out his arms to welcome them. "The grace of our Lord Jesus Christ, the love of God, and the fellowship of the Holy Spirit be with you."

"And also with you."

Patricia looked up at *Jesus, Light of the World*, and Michael, her Guardian angel. She had prayed for help; it had come to her; and she whispered her thanks.

Tim beamed at them, "Dearly Beloved, we have come together to pray for God's blessing on the marriage of Patricia and Anthony, and to share in their love."

Tiny reflections of candle flames winked in his glasses. "The gift of marriage brings together husband and wife, in good times and bad, to find strength and companionship in each other. We pray that the Holy Spirit will guide and strengthen Patricia and Anthony in their new life together. They have asked to repeat the words of their marriage commitment to each other in this sacred space, and in joy that you are here to witness them."

Patricia smiled comfortingly at Anthony's nerves as they faced each other and joined both hands. He had already said the words this morning, but St. Peter's was different. He was no longer a young man, but here, he was closest to his mother. He was introducing his bride.

"I, Anthony, take you, Patricia, to be my beloved wife. To have and to hold, from this day forward, for better, for worse, for richer, for poorer, in sickness and in health, to love and to cherish, till death do us part. According to God's Holy Law."

He smiled into her eyes as her voice softly echoed his. "I, Patricia, take you, Anthony, to be my beloved husband. To have and to hold, from this day forward, for better, for worse, for richer, for poorer, in sickness and in health, to love and to cherish, till death do us part. According to God's Holy Law."

Tim addressed them. "In the presence of God and this congregation, Anthony and Patricia have made their marriage commitment to each other. Those whom God has joined, let no one put asunder."

Patricia knelt at the altar rail with Anthony. She prayed they might have more happy times and face the challenges together. Until there was a cure, Parkinson's disease would gradually take Anthony's coordination and then, his life.

It was Christmas, a new beginning for them, for Matt at Newmarket, and for a baby, on its way to Clair and David. Next year, St. Peter's would have a noticeboard in the porch, alive with services and activities.

No one knows the exact ending of their life. Freedom comes from accepting that there are a few things you can control, and many that you cannot. Patricia knew that she could deal with whatever came, and her heart was at peace.

Audrey played the introduction to *Angels from the Realms of Glory,* and the music lifted Patricia's soul. She and Anthony would not be there for the Midnight Service at St. Mary's, it was too soon after the surgery. But they had been practicing this arrangement with the choir. Patricia held hands with Anthony and it felt right to take a deep breath and sing. Anthony's voice joined hers in their favorite carol.

Penny Appleton

Angels from the Realms of Glory,
Wing your flight o'er all the Earth,
Ye who sang Creation's story,
Now proclaim Messiah's birth.
Gloria, in excelsis deo!

Glory to God in the Highest
Amen.

Did you enjoy
A Summerfield
Christmas Wedding?

Thanks for joining Patricia and
Anthony in Summerfield Village.

If you enjoyed the book, a review would be much appreciated as it helps other readers discover the story.

More from Penny Appleton

Love, Second Time Around - Maggie and Greg's story.
A senior sweet romance.

Love Will Find a Way - Jenna and Dan's story

Love, Home at Last - Lizzie and Harry's story

Love at the Summerfield Stables - Clair and David's story

A Summerfield Christmas Wedding -
Patricia and Anthony's story. A senior sweet romance.

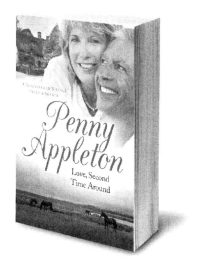

Scottish river, Maggie finds herself working in opposition to a man she once loved from afar, many years ago.

Idaho ranch owner Greg Warren is rich and entitled, with a dark past that he hides behind a professional smile. But inside, he struggles with loneliness after the loss of his wife and the rage of a wild daughter who won't let him move on.

Love blooms as Maggie and Greg take a chance on a new start, but can they find a balance between the two worlds they inhabit?

In this sweet romance, set between the English countryside and the wide expanse of the Idaho plains, can Maggie and Greg find love second time around?

Available now in ebook, print, and Large Print formats.

About Penny Appleton

Penny Appleton is the pen name of Jacqui Penn, a writer from the south-west of England.

Before she retired, Jacqui travelled in many countries and now enjoys visiting exciting places on vacation. She has been a volunteer for several organizations, including riding experiences for the disabled which features in Love at Summerfield Stables. Many of her stories contain aspects of her adventures and experiences.

Jacqui enjoys life and relishes variety. She loves walking in nature and the city, visiting National Trust properties and museums. She is an avid reader and is interested in wellness, yoga, and good nutrition.

Relationships, animals, and love, in all its myriad forms, are at the heart of her books.

Her favorite authors include Jane Austen, Danielle Steele and Nora Roberts. Also, Deborah Moggach, JoJo Moyes, and Suzanne Collins. Her favorite movies include *Pride and Prejudice*, *Salmon Fishing in the Yemen*, *The Best Exotic Marigold Hotel*, and *Me Before You*.

Acknowledgements

Thanks to my proofreader, Arnetta Jackson, and to Jane at JD Smith Design for the cover design and formatting.

Printed in Great Britain
by Amazon

56251713R00137